Damaged Grumpy Billionaire Daddy

Enemies to Lovers Second Chance Romance

By Kelly Thomas

Blank Slate Publications

BLANK SLATE
Publications

I crave to be back in his strong tattooed arms, but he can't ignore my past.

Seeing him as a daddy, and his loving devotion to our son, makes my heart melt.

Under his grumpy exterior is the man I remember - and I want him back.

When things heat up, my barriers fail.

His touch ignites an inferno, and I drop my defenses... and my panties.

I yearn for a second chance to repair his damaged heart.

If only he could forgive the secret that ripped us apart.

Contents

1. One   1

2. Two   12

3. Three   23

4. Four   34

5. Five   43

6. Six   54

7. Seven   62

8. Eight   73

9. Nine   84

10. Ten   95

11. Eleven   106

12.	Twelve	116
13.	Thirteen	127
14.	Fourteen	138
15.	Fifteen	150
16.	Sixteen	162
17.	Seventeen	173
18.	Eighteen	184
19.	Nineteen	195
20.	Twenty	207
21.	Twenty-One	218
22.	Twenty-Two	229
23.	Twenty-Three	239
24.	Twenty-Four	249
25.	Twenty-Five	260
26.	Twenty-Six	272
27.	Twenty-Seven	284
28.	Twenty-Eight	295
29.	Epilogue	309
Did you like this Book?		315

One

Carson

I glare at my brothers again, "What the hell do you mean? I need a life. I have a life. Dammit."

Carter, my middle brother, simply raises an eyebrow. While my youngest brother, Chase, who is four years my junior, lets out a snorting laugh. "Carson, you need a personal life," he clarifies, his tone suggesting I'm an imbecile. "Outside of work." My jaw tightens.

"I'm the CEO of this company for a reason," I retort, turning my glare on both of them. "I barely have time to get everything done as it is."

Carter points out, "We could hire a CFO to take care of all the paperwork and projections. That alone could take a lot off your plate. Leaving you to steer the company in the right direction."

"Thank you, Carter," I cut in dryly. "But the last time we hired someone, they were completely incompetent."

"And we understand that, but it's been a couple of years, and we think you should try again."

"I'll think about it," I mutter in a grumpy voice. I hold up my hand when they both look like they want to say more. "This is the end of our conversation. You can see yourselves out."

"Alright, Carson. Listen, we're going to try to get together at Wild Rider's this Friday. You up for it?" I see the hint of a challenge in their eyes.

"Sure. I'll be there. Around seven?"

That seems to appease them—for now. As they nod and then slowly leave my office.

After they're gone, I swivel my chair so I can look out my grand picture window. It gives me a magnificent view of the St. John's River as it meanders through Jacksonville on its way to the ocean. I have the best view in the building, and I know it. In fact, I planned it that way. I hand-picked this space on the second floor just for this view when the building was being built.

I let out a sigh as I idly track the slow-moving water. I know my brothers are right, but I won't tell them that. It has been a while since I've stepped away from the responsibilities here at work. It's been years since my last vacation. And I haven't hit the open road on my motorcycle in weeks. That used to be my temporary escape, but this last month has been hectic. By the time I get home, I normally just crash and unwind with a glass of scotch.

Absently, I pick up a pen, turning it over in my fingers as I continue gazing out the window. The rhythmic motion mirrors the swirling thoughts in my mind. Both of my brothers have recently found love, and now they're eager for me to share in their bliss. It's a shift from just Mom's well-meaning nudges – now Chase and Carter are pushing me to find someone special.

They know I haven't had the time or inclination for a real relationship. All I have the time for these days is fleeting connections—meaningless hookups.

The truth is, I never wanted the picket fence and a two-car garage. Never met a woman who ignited a spark strong enough to consider settling down... *That's a lie*; I hear the whisper in the back of my mind.

There was one. Her image surfaces even after all these years – thick chestnut hair framing clear gray eyes that seemed so innocent, so trustworthy. Eyes that lied and deceived me in a way that left a gaping wound.

The sting of betrayal flares anew, a bitter reminder. Damn her. She practically ruined me for anyone else. I shove the memory back, burying it deep within the guarded corners of my heart. It was a long time ago, a harsh lesson learned. I haven't let anyone close enough to risk getting hurt like that again.

I lean back in my desk chair as I think back over the recent years. No other woman has captured my attention long enough for me to try and make time for her in my busy schedule.

After my father died, I took over the business. The weight of responsibility settled heavily on my shoulders, pushing me to build it into the multi-billion-dollar company it is today. Funny, but the first billion was the hardest. After that, the business just kept its momentum, and now it's one of the most successful security companies in the nation. A fact that I am immensely proud of. I'd like to think my father would be proud of what I've accomplished. He groomed me for this role from a young age, ensuring the family legacy continued.

My brothers and I are all involved in the security industry. Chase trains our security guards, and Carter heads up our newest division of elite bodyguards. Even though travel used to be Carter's lifeblood, he committed to staying in town long enough to get the recruits trained and the entire division operational. He seems to have settled down a bit since finding Kat and putting a ring on her finger.

Chase and Val just had their first child—a daughter. I shake my head because I never would have thought Chase would end up a family man. But he seems content. Dammit, both my brothers do. While I—I'm not sure what I want anymore.

I swivel my chair away from the picture window. The river view is suddenly uninspiring, as it's doing little to diminish the growing sense of restlessness gnawing inside me. I'm bored with my current predictable lifestyle that doesn't leave room for anything or anyone else.

I'm weary of the same routine, the same empty nights, the same—emptiness. But what do I want? I can't even answer that question, as the 'what' remains frustratingly just out of reach. Lately, I've been craving something—different. I run my fingers through my hair as I scoff. Hell, I don't even know what different looks like.

I lean my elbows on my desk and turn toward my laptop and the never-ending emails awaiting my attention, pushing my contemplative thoughts away for now.

Suzanne, my admin, buzzes my desk phone. "Carson, there's a young man downstairs asking to see you."

"Did he say what he wants?"

"No, Clara at the reception desk just buzzed me. She did say she thought you should see him, but she didn't mention why."

I frown; Clara has been with the company since I was a boy. I trust her instincts. "Fine. Send him up."

I'm reading the first email when my admin knocks softly on the door. "Carson, the young man is here to see you."

"Alright, thanks."

As she turns away, a young, raw-boned boy with a backpack slung over his shoulders stands hesitantly in the doorway. But his eyes are boring holes in me. There's an unsettling familiarity about him: his dark hair and brows, the blue of his eyes. I feel like I should know him.

"Are you Carson Knight?" He bluntly asks.

"Yes," I give him a cool look as I take in his jeans, T-shirt, and tennis shoes, mentally cataloging every detail. "What brings you to Knight Security?"

I watch as he shuffles into my office. Instead of looking around, his gaze remains fixed on mine.

"You're my father."

I just about choke on a cough, "I'm sorry, what did you say?"

"You're my father." He says it with utter conviction. He puts his hand in his back pocket and pulls out a piece of paper. He shoves it at me as he says defensively, "That's what the DNA testing shows."

He walks toward my desk. I reach out, take the paper, and calmly read it over. Ever since our company was featured in Billionaire Tech magazine, all kinds of crackpots have made baseless claims.

"This report says there's a high probability that I'm your father." I point out dryly as I raise an eyebrow at him. "What's your mother's name, Boy?"

"My mom is Anna Johnson."

The blood drains from my face, and I suddenly feel light-headed. "Anna Johnson, is your mother?" I repeat in a stunned voice.

"Yeah." That's all he says, but he watches my face closely. Too closely. He probably saw how his words affected me. I'm suddenly finding it difficult to breathe.

"I have her picture," he says with a defensive lift of his chin. He walks over to a chair and slings his backpack onto the seat. Then he turns toward me as he pulls out his cell phone. He swipes a few times on the screen and turns the screen toward me.

I reach out with an unsteady hand. It looks like a recent picture or maybe just a few years old. Anna is standing behind the boy with a wide smile on her face, her hand on his shoulder. She looks—like a proud mother. My head swims, and I close my eyes for a minute.

"Hey, mister, you ain't gonna faint or something. Are you?" It sounds like he might be concerned.

I shake my head, but there's a ringing in my ears, so I gulp in a few quick breaths.

I look up, and the kid's eyes watch me closely. I give him a wan smile. "Why don't you sit down?"

He nods again and steps backward. Without removing his gaze, he slides the backpack to the floor and sits, all while maintaining eye contact. It's a little unnerving.

Neither one of us speaks for a few moments. I do the math and look at him with a cocked eyebrow, "How old are you?"

"I'm ten."

"You look older," I state quietly.

"Yeah." Another shrug.

"Where is your mother?"

Finally, I see a crack in his demeanor. He wipes his palms over his knees, a sign of nervousness.

"She doesn't know I'm here." His eyes drop to the floor. "I skipped school to find you."

"Where do you live?" I ask him slowly, trying to recover.

"We just moved to Orlando a few days ago. We're from Ft. Lauderdale."

"So, how did you get here?" I ask, curious.

He looks uncomfortable at my question, "I took the bus. Alone."

"I wouldn't think you could travel alone. I thought you had to be thirteen—"

He sighs, "Nah. You have to be twelve, but I'm tall for my age. They believed me." He shrugs.

Ten and taking a bus alone, I think to myself; a wave of surprise and concern washes over me. This kid's got guts, that's for sure. I run my eyes over him again, checking him out. He is indeed tall for his age if he's only ten. But then, so was I when I was his age.

I glance at my watch. It's eleven thirty. "I think we should call your mother."

He gives me a stubborn look, but I can see a glint of worry behind his eyes. "I will. But I... um... I wanted to see you. Talk to you first."

I nod. I can tell the boy is not done, so I don't try to rush him.

"Did you know about me?" As he asks the question, his chin comes up, and I can tell he's trying to act like it doesn't matter, but I see the look of vulnerability in his eyes.

So, I tell him the truth. "No. If you are my son..." I take a deep breath. I'm only learning about it now from you."

That appears to satisfy him, and he gives a quick nod.

"If your mother thinks you're at school. When will she be expecting you? I don't want her to worry."

He suddenly frowns, and I can tell the thought of his mother worrying about him bothers him; he tries to cover it up with a shrug.

"The school bus drops off at three thirty."

"I think we need to call her," I state more firmly. I wait as he thinks it over.

"Alright," he agrees with a bit of reluctance. With his phone in his hand, he just sits there looking down at it.

I stand and walk over to him. "Do you want me to call her?"

"Yeah, would you?" He hands over his phone willingly with a relieved twist of his lips.

I take the phone, and in his favorites, I see 'Mom.' Before I make the call, I look down at him. "What's your name?"

"Connor." And then, in a move that surprises me, I reach down and place my hand reassuringly on his shoulder.

Two

Anna

I look around the rental with a grimace. There are moving boxes piled high. I give a heartfelt sigh. I was hoping to be further along in the unpacking by now, but my heart isn't in it. We've had so many problems with this move.

When my cell phone rings, it takes me a few minutes to locate it among all the boxes and packing material strewn across the room. I grab it up once I find it on the floor beside an open box.

I see it's Connor, "Hey, Connor. What's up?"

"Anna, it's Carson Knight." My heart drops, and I reach out a hand to steady myself. "Your son showed up here at Knight Security a little while ago. He claims I'm his father, and he has a DNA report with him."

I sink weakly onto the floor because the new chairs haven't arrived yet, and my legs won't support me.

"I... Carson, Is he okay?"

"Yes, he's fine. He came by bus."

"Where? Um— you're in Jacksonville, Florida?"

"Yes."

"I'll leave within the hour."

"Okay. Anna, no need to hurry. He's safe. We'll talk once you get here." I can hear the unspoken accusation in his voice through the phone. I nod weakly, even though he can't see me. "We'll be at my place when you arrive. I'll text you the address."

"Thank you," I say weakly. He doesn't say goodbye; he just disconnects the call.

I shut my eyes as my head reels. Carson. Carson Knight. The father of my son and the man who refuses to forgive me.

As I dazedly start to pull myself to my feet, I remember his words, no need to hurry, Connor is safe. So, I remain in my position on the floor. I lean my heavy head back against an unopened box and shut my eyes.

Carson, it's easy to remember him as I only have to look in my son's eyes to see Carson's face, his intense blue eyes. Connor even has some of his mannerisms, the way he cocks an eyebrow at me. I bite my lip as tears gather at the back of my eyes.

How many years has it been? Connor is ten, so it's been eleven years since the cruise— since I met Carson. I let the memories intrude.

I didn't want to go on a cruise by myself. But I was urged to go. The trip was a gift. So, I went.

That very first night, the cruise line organized a masquerade party for everyone on board. They had complimentary masks available. I remember picking out a blue and black lace mask.

The ballroom was crowded. Everyone was drinking and eating. It was festive and more fun than I thought it would be. I remember someone said something funny, and I threw back my head and laughed out loud. We were all anonymous. No one knew me. I could relax and let the stress of the previous six months roll off me.

When I raised my head, I felt eyes on me. I looked around until I found him. He was staring, and he had on the masculine version of my blue and black mask. His eyes burned into me, even from a distance. I shivered from the sensual look in his eyes. He was leaning back against the wall with his arms crossed over his chest. He wore a white dress shirt with the sleeves rolled up. Showing off a couple of tattoos. He looked cocky and dangerous.

When he straightened and walked toward me, I realized how tall he was. How muscular. He exuded a masculine charm even with his face covered. When he reached my side, we talked. We danced. I guess I felt safe behind my mask. I would never have acted so carefree with him, as I did otherwise.

It was later, much later when he walked me to my cabin. He leaned down and kissed me. And I let him. To this day, I don't think I could have stopped myself. I wanted him to kiss me. And Lordy, did that man know how to kiss.

He took his time. He leaned me back against the door and held my face between his hands. He tilted my face up and nibbled on my lower lip, then the corners, and the top. When he sucked on my lower lip, I gasped, and he smoothly delved in. He explored my mouth slowly like he wanted to savor me. I remember feeling breathless. When I blinked open my eyes, my hands were around his neck, and I was pressed up against him. He towered over me.

He reached out with a hand and cupped my cheek. He kissed me one more time, a slow, thorough kiss that sent shivers down my spine. He looked up at my cabin number and smiled. Looking down at me, he whispered, "I'll be seeing you around."

Then he left, his scent lingering, invading my every breath—I could still feel his strong arms around me. I stood there leaning against the door until I heard someone approaching. I slowly turned and opened my cabin door, and stepped inside. It took me a good hour before I could sleep, my dreams filled with the image of a tall, dark, and handsome masked man.

I blink a few times to chase away the old memories. Opening my eyes to the present, I look around at the mess and pull myself up from the floor. I make my way into the bedroom that is going to be mine and shake my head. My clothes are all still in boxes.

The movers were supposed to be handling all of this. I look over at my suitcase, which is what I've been living out of for the past three days. At least I won't have to pack much more into it. I slowly move around the cluttered apartment, picking up everything I think I'll need for a couple of days away.

I check Connor's room, but it looks like he took what he needed. He's resourceful. He made it all the way to Jacksonville by himself. He's ten years old, going on thirty, half the time.

I wheel my suitcase to the door and turn out all the lights. I punch in the address Carson texted me, into my GPS to get directions. Once I'm on the road, there's nothing to hold back the memories. They insistently push against my awareness. I finally silence the radio and give in to the pressing memories.

It was the next morning after the masquerade party... after that unforgettable kiss. I chose to get breakfast in the main room, where they served buffet style. After I filled my plate and grabbed a steaming cup of coffee, I sat down at a vacant table.

I tried not to think of the kiss, of him. But I wondered what he looked like under the mask. Would I recognize him if I ever saw him again?

A shadow fell across the table, and I looked up. It was as if I had conjured him. He was even more handsome than I had imagined. The dark hair and his intense blue eyes were recognizable from the night before. His lean cheeks and chiseled jaw made me inhale so fast I almost choked. I cleared my throat while he stood there over me with an easy grin, holding a tray laden with food.

"Can I sit?" His voice had the same deep tone as the night before.

I wordlessly nodded, wondering if I should allow him to eat with me. I felt the need to keep my distance.

"How... how did you recognize me?" I asked with genuine curiosity as he sat down.

"You're hair and your smile."

"My hair? It's brown. A mousy brown color."

"No. Mousy brown? Absolutely not. It's more of a chestnut color and lighter around your face. It's long and cascades in waves over your shoulders."

His words, almost poetic, had me glancing over at him. I thought he might be mocking me, but instead, his eyes were still on my hair. The admiring look in his eyes gave me a warm feeling. I also felt a warmth in my cheeks as I blush easily.

I quickly looked away. "Okay, because it would have been kind of creepy if you had been waiting for me to exit my cabin."

He threw back his head and laughed at my words, "Well, I did think of that, but it was going to be my last resort if I couldn't find you this morning," He admitted with a grin.

As we ate our breakfast together, we talked casually about the weather and the ports we'd be visiting soon.

Once we were finished, he reached out and put his hand over mine, "Anna?" I discretely pulled my hand away. But the look in his eyes and that masculine smile caused a hitch in my breath, as did his next words.

"Why don't we spend the day together?" He asked.

I instantly started to shake my head, "No. I—"

"Oh, come on. It could be fun." He had such a persuasive look on his face.

I shook my head firmly, "No. Thank you. We're still at sea, and I already made plans to laze by the pool and sunbathe. I brought lots of books and promised myself I'd just be lazy and read."

He accepted my answer with a nod and shrug. "I'm disappointed, but I understand. Besides, tomorrow is when we will pull into the port. I won't take another no quite so easily." He warned me with a smile and a promising glint in his eye.

Then he picked up his tray and walked away. I was relieved, but a wave of disappointment caught me by surprise at how easily he had given up. I reminded myself of my plans and that I should be glad he left so quickly.

After I changed into my swimsuit, grabbed a coverall, and my filled beach bag, I made my way to the outside deck. It was such a beautiful day. The sun shone, there was a strong sea breeze, and everywhere I looked, people were enjoying themselves. I smiled. I was glad that I was there. I spread out on a lounger and settled in to read.

A few hours later, I felt his eyes on me. I shivered at the awareness. I cautiously raised my head, and there he was in bright white and orange board shorts. His tanned chest showed off his defined abs. His shoulders were broad and muscular. His white smile against his tanned face made my mouth go dry. He just flashed me a grin and jumped into the pool.

He kept his distance that entire day, but I couldn't help but notice how many of the single girls sat up and took notice of him.

I resolutely put my nose in my book. If my eyes wandered in his direction every so often, who could blame me? The guy was eye candy at its best. Soon, a group of single guys and girls were all hanging out together. I could hear their bright laughter from where I sat alone with my book.

The next morning at breakfast, I was surprised to find him asking to join me again.

I don't remember what the conversation was about. All I remember is laughing and smiling and how much I enjoyed just talking with him. So, when he asked me if we could leave the ship together, I nodded my acceptance. It was only after he left that I sat there, berating myself for agreeing to spend more time with him.

We had a good time wandering through the stalls in the Bahamas. George Town, Grand Cayman. I truly tried to keep my distance.

I remember when he first grabbed my hand as we walked through a very crowded section of Grand Cayman. As soon as we cleared the crowd, I pulled my hand from his. He turned to me with a small frown. "Hey, are you okay?"

"Yes, I... Look, Carson. I'm not interested in anything more than friendship. A platonic friendship," I finished firmly, coming to a dead stop.

"Okay. I apologize if I came on too strong—"

"No, Carson, it's nothing you've done. It's me. I... I've been dealing with some very stressful things. I didn't even want to come on this vacation. But I was given the tickets as a gift and told to go and enjoy myself. So, I did. I came, and I'm enjoying myself. But I didn't plan on enjoying this trip with anyone else. I needed some alone time."

He nodded solemnly. "I get that. I tell you what. Tomorrow, we're at sea again, and I promise to leave you alone. Give you some space. However, I would like to tour Cozumel with you when we arrive. Deal?"

I hesitated, but looking up at him being so understanding, I finally caved. "Alright. Thanks for not pushing me."

We spent the rest of that day laughing and just enjoying the sights. Carson was so easy to be with. Whenever he asked me about myself, I would shrug or give him a vague answer. It didn't take him long to take the hint, but every once in a while, I would feel his eyes on me as if I were a puzzle. An enigma. He kept trying to figure out why I was so hesitant to confide in him.

Someone blares their horn. As the car in front of me on the highway swerves, pulling my attention from the past. I blink as I look around at the cars. The traffic's gotten heavier. I pass a sign showing how many miles till I arrive in Jacksonville. I'm halfway there.

Three

Carson

I disconnect the call. Text my address to Anna, and hand the phone back to Connor—my son.

"Your Mom is on her way. It's about a three-hour drive. Are you hungry?"

"Yeah." He practically jumps out of the chair and turns to face me. He's tall. As I look at him, I feel my throat tighten with emotion. Anna didn't deny that he is my son. She also didn't confirm it. But as my eyes meet his, it's uncanny. It's as if my own reflection is staring back at me from a younger time.

I suddenly reach out, grab his shoulders, and pull him toward me. I think I startled him as I feel him stiffen, but then, as my arms wrap around him, he sags against my chest. I continue to hug him to me tightly. I feel like the Grinch as I swear my heart expands to three times its size.

We stand like that for a few minutes. Finally, I loosen my hold, and he steps back. I pretend not to see the sheen in his eyes. My own are suspiciously wet, as well. I reach out and purposely ruffle his hair, something I hated my parents to do. I do it just to break the poignancy of the moment. It works as he gives a lopsided grin and ducks back out of reach.

"Come on, let's go grab a burger," I say with a grin.

As we walk past my admin's desk, Suzanne looks up curiously. Her wide eyes go from me to the preteen at my side. I'm not ready yet to discuss this with anyone. It's too new, too personal, too overwhelming.

I keep my face blank as I say, "I'll need you to cancel my appointments for today." I stop and glance over at Connor. "Actually, I'll need you to cancel everything for the rest of the week."

She nods like the request is not that unusual and offers me a small smile. "Of çourse, Carson. I'll ensure you're not disturbed for the rest of the week."

"Thanks. We're going to lunch now, and I won't be back this afternoon. I'll give you a call tomorrow to discuss my schedule. Thanks, Suzanne."

"Carson, please don't worry about a thing. Nothing is pressing that I or your brothers can't handle." I nod my thanks as Connor follows me into the elevator.

I drive to a restaurant near the office that's known for its burgers. Once we get in the car, Connor stows his backpack in the backseat. As I drive out of the parking garage, Connor looks around the interior of the car.

"Nice ride," he says lightly.

I grin, "Thanks."

We walk into the restaurant and take a seat. When the waitress comes around, Connor orders a double cheeseburger with fries and a soda.

"I'll take the same but with onion rings and an iced tea," I say as I hand her the menus.

After the waitress leaves, Connor puts his elbows on the table and props up his chin as he looks around, then glances back at me like he doesn't quite know what to say.

"So, tell me about yourself. How's school? What type of sports are you into?" I smile as that seems to be all the incentive he needs.

He grins and starts slowly, but soon, he's talking quickly as he starts to open up.

"My friend Jeff, he's back in Lauderdale. He and I used to shoot hoops after school. Next year, I'll be in Junior High, but in Orlando."

"Why did you move from Ft. Lauderdale to Orlando?"

"Mom wanted a change." He shrugs his shoulders, "She's been wanting to move out of Lauderdale for years. She said our house was a maus... mausa... you know, like a museum."

"A mausoleum?"

"Yeah, that's what she called it. Said it felt like a tomb."

"It was just you and your mom?" I ask carefully.

"Yeah. Mom and I lived in one wing of the house. Graham used to live in the other until he died."

The waitress delivers our meals. After she leaves, I watch as a starving Connor takes a massive bite out of his cheeseburger, scoops up a handful of fries, and devours them. Next, he reaches for the ketchup and squirts out a hefty helping onto his plate. After that, he drags each french fry through the ketchup before placing it in his mouth.

"Graham? Did he raise you?" I ask gruffly.

"Nah, well, I mean... I kinda remember him. He was nice and all, but he was always sick. Mom was constantly taking care of him." Connor looks up at me curiously, "Did you know him?"

"No. I never met the man," I say in a tight voice.

"Well, Mom wanted to move right after he died, but it took a long time for his estate to be settled. It was weird. One day, when I got home from school, Mom said she'd put the house up for sale and that we were moving. Then we did."

"What made you get the DNA testing?"

Connor frowns down at a now-drowning french fry. He picks it up, gets ketchup all over his fingers, and pops it in his mouth. He licks the remaining ketchup off his fingers, leaving a smear on his chin.

Finally, he answers, "I was going through a box of Graham's stuff. A bunch of old papers, some journals, and legal junk. It was in this bright yellow box." He makes a face and gestures with his hands, "Anyway, inside the box, I found a picture of you and my mom. She looked really happy. I asked her who you were." He looks up at me solemnly, "She didn't answer me at first. But then she told me that she hurt you really badly and that you didn't want her in your life."

Connor stops and glances over at me, a hint of wistfulness shining in his eyes. "I picked up the picture, and I kinda look like you. I figured you might be my dad. So, I sent away for a DNA kit."

He gives me a curious look, "Was that true?"

"Was what true, Connor?"

"That my mom hurt you and that you don't want her in your life anymore?" He tilts his head to the side as he waits for my answer.

"Yes, she hurt me. And because of that, we can never have a future together."

His eyes widen at my words, and he solemnly nods, "It must have been pretty bad."

"It was, but that's all I can tell you. Your Mom would have to tell you the rest if she wants to." I wipe my mouth and hands with a paper napkin and toss it down on my now-empty plate.

I look over at his plate, which only has crumbs. "You ready to go?"

"Sure," he answers with another shrug. I hide a grin as I wonder if I ever shrugged as often as he does. I have a feeling I did.

After we're in the SUV and I'm pulling away, he asks, "Where are we going now?"

I look at him across the car's interior. "My apartment. We can hang out there until your mother arrives."

"Okay," is his answer. I reach down and turn on the radio to one of the local rock radio stations. I turn up the volume and watch Connor as he nods his head to the beat of the rock song.

When I drive into the parking garage, he looks around. He follows me into the elevator, and we ride up to the penthouse. The elevator delivers us to the hall outside my front door.

"Cool," Is all that he says as I open the door to my apartment. When Connor walks in with his backpack, my eyes follow him. I see him stop and look around; the three-bedroom, two-bath apartment is spacious, with high ceilings. At one end of the living room are triple glass sliding doors that open onto an expansive balcony where you can watch the evening sunset. I have another magnificent view of the St. John's River.

"Wow, your view here is almost as nice as the one in your office."

I smile, "I agree. The view from my office is better. This one is just more panoramic."

I watch as he throws down his backpack and then checks out all the rooms. I follow him. He finally slows down when he gets to the bedrooms. "This place is huge."

A few minutes later, "I gotta take a leak," and he heads to the main bathroom.

I smile as I've almost forgotten what it's like to be around a preteen boy. That stops me in my tracks. He's almost a teenager, and I've missed ten years of his life. Ten whole years.

The unjustness of it all clogs my throat. I want to yell in frustration and punch a hole in the wall. How could she keep something so important from me? Why didn't Anna tell me?

Then I remember our last conversation. I told her not to contact me. That I never wanted to see or hear from her again. I said she was dead to me. And I meant every word. But still, a son? She should have told me she carried my son. I have to hide my smoldering emotions from Connor when I hear him make his way down the hall.

He suddenly spies a basketball in the spare bedroom. "You play hoops?" I hear him ask from the other room.

"Yeah, my brothers and I still play one-on-one, but there's a hoop on the ground floor. Wanna shoot a few while we wait for your mom?"

When he doesn't answer, I walk into the spare bedroom to discover him perched on the bed, absorbed in the wall-mounted family portrait featuring my parents, myself, and my two brothers.

"Hey, Connor, you okay?"

He turns toward me but doesn't stand. His face has an unreadable look, but his eyes seem to bulge. "I have uncles?" I hear the wonder in his voice.

I sit down on the edge of the bed beside him, and I point to the picture, "That was my dad, your grandpa. He died before I met your mother. The lady beside him is your grandma, my mother. Her name is Bonnie. She will cry when she meets you." He just smiles and blinks rapidly. "I'm the oldest, but this is Carter, my middle brother who's engaged to a woman named

Kat. They both work at the office you were at. Carter travels a lot, but he recently set up and trained our elite bodyguard division."

I point again to the picture on the wall. "The other guy is my youngest brother, Chase. He's married, and his wife's name is Val. They have a little girl named Gabriella."

I stop and smile at him, "So let's see. You have a grandma, two uncles, two aunts, and a baby girl cousin."

"Wow, the only family I've ever had was my mom. She doesn't have anyone, either. You have a really big family."

"And now you do, too." I wink at him as I nod toward the picture, "My dad was one of eight siblings, so that's just your immediate family. There are so many Knights around this town, you won't be able to count them all." I laugh as his eyes bulge again, but I can see the anticipation of meeting them shining bright.

I go over to the desk in the spare bedroom and pull out a family album that my mother gave me on my last birthday. I hand it to Connor as we open it. I figured he'd soon grow bored with the endless pictures, but I watch as he eagerly asks about each photo. The last section of the album is pictures from one of our family cookouts. He's like a sponge wanting to know who is who and how they're related to him.

We finish the last page, and I tell him about my brother's boat and the boathouse when the doorbell rings. I watch as the smile disappears from his face, and he turns toward me. His voice is barely above a whisper, "My mom's gonna be mad."

I awkwardly wrap my arm around his shoulders and say gruffly, "Maybe, but she loves you, and she'll just be relieved that you're safe."

Four

Anna

My hand raises, and I ring the doorbell, hearing the sound of chimes faintly through the thick door. Taking a deep breath, I try to control the frantic beating of my heart. I try to uncoil the knot of dread that settled in my stomach ever since I got Carson's phone call.

I wipe my damp palms down my jeans and try to keep them from shaking. Oh, God. What possessed Connor to come here? Alone? I know he's been yearning for a male presence in his life, but he's only ten. Anything could have happened to him on that bus ride.

And let's face it, the dull ache in my chest is from a blend of hurt and anger. My son kept this visit a secret and came to see his father, a complete stranger, by himself.

The door suddenly swings open. Nothing could have lessened the impact of seeing Carson again. The air catches in my throat, and my heart continues to pound loudly in my chest. I feel like I'm about to faint as my head swims and my eyes rise to meet his.

They are the same piercing blue and hold no warmth or hint of softened emotions after all these years. In fact, they seem colder, harder, like chips of ice as they rake over me.

He steps back, gesturing for me to enter the apartment.

My gaze darts to Connor, his small frame standing hesitantly beside his father. Relief washes over me as I rush toward him.

I wrap my arms around him and give him a hard hug. As I hold him close, I steal a glance at the man beside him. The years have added lines around his eyes, his dark hair is the same but in a different style. If anything, he's broader now, his form sculpted with hard muscles that weren't there before.

I turn as I step back, my hands still on Connor's shoulders, and take a good look at my son. I have to ensure that he's okay.

I guess I take too long because he gives one of his signature shrugs, trying to dislodge my grasp.

I let my hands fall to my sides while a sense of dread, heavy and cold, settles in my stomach. Then, with reluctance and a deep breath, I turn slowly toward his father.

Carson's face looks carved from granite as he states quietly, "Let's all have a seat." I follow him into a contemporary living room decorated in warm, neutral tones of beige and brown.

I tentatively sit down on a buttery, soft brown leather sectional. Connor lowers his lanky frame beside me. Carson sits across from us in a matching armchair.

My mouth feels painfully dry as I try to gather my thoughts. The words I prepared on my way here have disappeared scattered, and my mind is a blank slate.

Carson leans forward, picks up a piece of paper from the coffee table in front of us, and hands it to me. I take it, my vision blurring as the words swim on the page. It's the DNA report. When I glance up again, I notice two pairs of eyes focused intently on my face. Both Connor and Carson stand. Waiting.

I lick my lips and state in a voice that barely wavers, "Connor is our son. You're his father."

I watch as Carson closes his eyes for a long moment. When he opens them, they're filled with a whirlwind of emotion. He turns to Connor, who approaches him cautiously. They both stop just a foot or two away from each other. Their gazes study each other with a solemn intensity.

As Carson pulls our son into an embrace, I hear Connor mutter, "Don't mess up my hair this time." I see Carson's lips twitch as he holds back a smile. Their emotional reunion clearly happened before I arrived. I swallow the bitter disappointment that knowledge gives me. Until now, it's just been me and my son, weathering the highs and lows together.

My breath catches in my throat as I realize our entire lives are about to change.

I've lived with my fear, wondering what would happen if Carson ever found out about Connor. Surely, he wouldn't keep my son from me. I feel the fear raise its ugly head again as I witness the bond forming so easily between them. I swallow it down. I can't deny them this closeness.

A boy needs his father. I frown at the unease of keeping them apart, but it's not like Carson was open to communicating with me. I push the wave of guilt to the back of my mind and paste a smile on my face. I blink to keep the wetness on my lashes from falling. I draw in another shaky breath.

Once Carson loosens his hold, he keeps his arm around Connor's shoulders as they turn toward me.

"Can we eat now?" Connor asks with a hopeful glance at me and his father, "Aren't you guys hungry?"

I see the smile spread across Carson's face before he openly chuckles, "You're a growing boy. I was always hungry at your age, too."

They both turn and give me identical looks of raised eyebrows. "I could eat. Did you have something here for me to fix, or are we going out?" I ask.

"Out," Carson answers with a grin, "Then, after dinner, we can run by a store and pick up some groceries for breakfast." He turns toward Connor, "What do you like in the mornings?"

Connor shrugs and answers honestly, "Anything. I love pancakes and bacon. I can eat cereal, too, if that's all you have. But I don't like oatmeal."

Carson nods, "Sorry, no cereal here, but you'll have to tell me what you like, and we'll get a box."

As we exit the apartment, Connor is listing his favorite cereals out loud. "Cap'n Crunch is good, and Cinnamon Toast Crunch. But no shredded wheat, not even the frosted kind..."

I grab my purse and follow them out to the elevator. Once we reach the parking garage, Connor piles into Carson's sleek black SUV, and he automatically gets in the back seat. Leaving the front passenger seat for me. Carson holds the door, but we avoid looking at each other as I murmur a quick thank you.

"Does anybody have a preference?" Carson asks as he pulls out into the Jacksonville traffic.

I shake my head, but Connor is more vocal. "How about barbecue? I can put away some ribs."

Carson smiles and turns the car, "I know just the place. He drives us to a restaurant called Mojo Bar-B-Que. We slide into a wooden booth. I sit beside Connor, and Carson slides in opposite us.

We all order ribs, and when our meals arrive, Connor actually stops his eager chatter as he's too busy eating. I look over at my son fondly as the boy devours his ribs as if he hasn't eaten in days, the sauce clinging to his cheeks, and he offers a sticky smile. I watch him lick his fingers with gusto.

I glance up to find Carson's eyes on me, "Do you like the ribs?"

"Yes, almost as much as Connor does," I say with a small smile. We both look over at Connor, who is finishing his ribs, while Carson and I have barely put a dent in our dinners.

After we leave the restaurant, we make a quick detour to a nearby grocery store. Later, we exit with a few bags of groceries and load them into the SUV. They are mostly breakfast foods, but I also grabbed some healthy snacks and a not-so-healthy bag of chips for Connor.

At Carson's questioning look, I explained with a slight smile, "Connor can eat you out of house and home."

Carson lets out a silent chuckle, a glint of amusement shimmering in his eyes as they track Connor. Our son, with youthful energy, volunteered to return the shopping cart. He can turn anything into an adventure, as he shoves it with all his might towards the corral. Then he jumps onto the back. The cart lurches forward, carrying him on a short, happy ride before it comes to rest with a soft bump.

Back in the apartment, I help Carson put away the food. Both of us are silent as we listen to Connor in the next room. Carson gave him carte blanche to pick out some music. My son has some very eclectic tastes. While he likes the typical Hip Hop, he also likes Rock and even older Rock artists and songs. We hear him softly debating over Pink Floyd or Imagine Dragons.

We both smile as we hear the beginning cords of a song from Pink Floyd's The Wall.

I sit off to the side while Carson and Connor eagerly debate the merits of the different bands. I'm content to listen to their animated discussions.

As eight o'clock approaches, Connor is already yawning, so Carson shows him to one of the spare bedrooms.

Carson instructs Connor in a low and soothing voice, "You can sleep in here. Your mother will be right next door." He gives a soft smile as he points with his thumb, "I'll be down the hall if you need anything."

Connor, his eyes heavy with sleep, manages a mumbled "Okay" before he gives in to a full yawn.

Carson turns to me, his gaze unreadable. "You can sleep in here, Anna."

I give a forced smile, "Thank you," my voice betraying my nerves, "I'll just get my stuff." I turn and wheel in my suitcase that my son brought up for me earlier.

A few minutes later, Connor emerges wearing a mismatched combination of shorts and the well-worn T-shirt he favors for sleeping. We follow him into the spare bedroom, the space suddenly charged with a strange tension.

I lean down and press a soft kiss on Connor's forehead. Then I turn to leave but find myself stopping to look back while I stand in the doorway. Unable to tear my eyes from the scene unfolding between my son and his father. This is the first time Carson will tuck Connor in. It's a simple act, but it feels monumental and charged with emotion.

Carson leans down and gives him a light kiss on the cheek. He reaches out to ruffle Connor's hair, a small gesture that speaks volumes. A lump forms in my throat, and my eyes burn with unshed tears as Carson murmurs, "Goodnight, Son."

I quickly turn and walk back into the living room. I stand there gulping in the air with my hand over my heart. I try to shake off the heavy emotions as I don't want to appear weak when Carson and I talk. And we will talk. I guess I should feel thankful that Carson was willing to wait for Connor to be in bed before we have this difficult conversation.

I slip off my shoes and pull my legs up beside me on the sofa. I wonder what's taking Carson so long. Wearily, I rest my head on the arm of the sofa as I wait for Carson.

Five

Carson

After I tuck in my son, he closes his eyes, rolls over, and wraps his arms around a pillow. I stand there, my eyes studying his small form. He looks so young with his eyes closed, his dark lashes resting peacefully on his cheeks.

I rub the back of my hand over my damp eyes. I can't believe the overwhelming emotions I feel as I look down at him. I feel like I should stand here and ward off any nightmares. Protect him from any unseen threats. My heart feels like it could burst with the love I feel bubbling up inside my chest.

I walk over to the lone armchair and sit down, my gaze remaining on my son's sleeping form. As I watch him, my mind goes back in time...

It wasn't Cozumel, but it was someplace in Mexico where I tried to kiss Anna again. We had already shared a kiss after the masquerade party, so I didn't think she would object. I was wrong.

We were sitting in a restaurant, we had just finished lunch, and we had enjoyed the day and each other's company. She took joy in the simplest things, like the bright flowers that grew on the side of the roads. She was fun to be around, and I couldn't believe how easy she was to talk to. We talked about everything from movies to music and books. She impressed me with her willingness to listen to every side of an argument or opinion. She was quick-witted but also quick to smile. In short, I couldn't wait to spend my days with her and was hoping we'd soon be spending our nights together.

When she settled back after finishing her dinner, I looked over at her, and she looked so adorable. She gave a small pout, and her cheeks were rosy from the bright sun as we had spent the day wandering through the Mexican streets. I couldn't help it; I leaned over and gave her a quick kiss. For a moment, she returned the kiss. Then, she was furiously pushing me away.

"Carson, I told you. I... I can't!"

I gave her a confused look, "Why not? What would it hurt? I like you, Anna." I looked directly into her clear gray eyes, "I like you a lot."

"No. Carson, we... I can't. Look, if we can't keep this platonic, then we'll have to stop spending time together. Understand?" She looked up at me with such a helpless, distraught look that I would have promised her anything. So, against my wishes, I agreed. "Okay, I'll keep my hands to myself. If that's what you want." My eyes bore into hers, looking for answers.

She nodded her head firmly, "Yes. That's what I want. That's the way it has to be, Carson."

"Alright, alright," I held up my hands in surrender, "I don't understand, but if that's the way you want it. Fine." I looked moodily away, then swung my eyes back to her.

I felt her gaze search my face. She finally nodded again. "Okay. Thank you, Carson." As I opened my mouth to ask another question, she stopped me with a raised hand. "No, no questions. Please. Just let it be. I can only tell you that my life is complicated right now."

"I'm sorry. I... I shouldn't have pushed you." I abruptly stand, "Come on, it's getting late. Let's get back to the ship."

I started to reach out my hand to help her up and caught myself. I fisted my hand instead and turned away. A few steps later, she caught up with me. She was biting her lip and looking miserable, but she fell in step beside me with her head down, and we walked silently back to the cruise line.

The girl had me all tied up in knots. The more time I spent with her, the more I wanted her. I ran my hand through my hair in frustration. I could be patient. I felt she'd be worth the wait—

I hear a soft, childish snore, and it nudges me back to the present time. My eyes go directly to Connor. He's sound asleep. I stand and smile down at him once more. I turn firmly, closing his bedroom door behind me.

I straighten, my features hardening as I think about the coming conversation with Anna. I stride purposefully into the living room to confront her. Determined to get answers on why she's kept my son a secret all this time.

My hands clench into fists, but then I see her. She's curled up on the couch, her bare feet tucked up underneath her. Her head is resting on the arm of the sofa. She's as sound asleep as our ten-year-old in the other room and looks almost as innocent. Looks can be deceiving, I think, with a grimace.

I heave a defeated sigh and sit down with a determination to wait her out. I'm sitting opposite her on the armchair as my eyes rove over her form. With her eyes closed, I look my fill. My eyes wander down to her full breasts and her tiny waist that flares out to shapely hips. I can't see all of her legs, but I remember them as long and shapely.

I shift on the chair, sit back, and with my brooding eyes on her, I drift once again into the past...

I think back to our time on the ship. I thought I had been patient long enough. I had been gentle and understanding. Yet, every time I tried getting close to her, she would back away. I was frustrated, physically and emotionally. I was tired of taking cold showers every night. I was tired of waiting. I wanted her, and the urge to claim her only increased every moment we spent together.

The cruise line was throwing another party. This time, it wasn't a masquerade, but most of the people dressed up. I again had on dress pants and a white dress shirt with the sleeves rolled up. When I knocked on her cabin, she came to the door in a simple white sundress. Her shoulders were tanned and glowing from our time in the sun. She looked beautiful, and my body hardened just looking at her. Her chestnut hair gleamed from the overhead light above us.

I held out my arm, and she smiled up at me as she placed her arm in mine. We heard the music playing as we approached. When we stepped onto the main deck, there was already a crowd. Plenty of drink and food, so typical of a cruise. I couldn't wait to pull her into my arms. As the music slowed, we swayed under the canopy of lights. She felt so good in my arms, but when I tried to pull her closer, she again resisted me.

I frowned down at her in confusion. "Why do you always pull away from me?"

I saw her close her eyes, and when she opened them, she bit her lip, "I... there's something I need to tell you—" Her words were cut off when someone almost knocked us down. I looked around at the half-drunken crowd. "Come on, let's go somewhere private."

We walked around to the front of the ship, but everywhere we walked, we found more people. Everyone seemed to have the same idea as us.

"Come on, let's go to your cabin, it's closer." She kept her head down as I led the way to her cabin.

Once we were inside, I immediately took her into my arms, and she again gently pushed me away.

"Anna, what is it?" I suddenly glance down at her, "Are you a virgin?"

I see her grin as she shakes her head, "No, Carson. That's not it. I'm..."

I suddenly can't wait a moment longer. I lean down and kiss her hungrily, and this time, when she puts up her hands, she doesn't hold me back for long. As I deepened the kiss, I felt the moment she surrendered. She pushed against me as her arms went around my neck. I felt her fingers in my hair, and I heard her soft sigh as I nuzzled her cheek.

"Oh, Carson, I—" But, I didn't want to talk, didn't want to listen. I only wanted her. She was finally not pushing me away. I took advantage and skimmed my hands over her slender form. I quickly divested her of her sundress. She stood before me in white panties, no bra. She gasped as I touched her breasts. Then, my mouth replaced my hands. She started to pant as I sucked on a nipple. Her hands tugged on my hair, but it was to keep me in place this time.

I slipped my hand between her legs and found her wet for me. I slipped in a finger; she was so tight. I worked her slowly. I heard her breathless moan as I managed to slip in another finger, priming her to take me. I'm large, and she felt so small and fragile in my arms.

I felt like a dam had burst. She was finally allowing me to touch her, hold her, and make love to her. I watched her clear gray eyes, like deep pools, turn cloudy with her desire. I felt her first tremors, and she shattered in my arms with a low keening sound.

I grinned triumphantly down at her. I stripped in record time, grabbing a condom from my pocket. Without letting her recover or come down from her high, I carried her swiftly to the bed and followed her down. I eagerly spread her legs wider with my thigh. When she opened her mouth, I placed my hand over her lips and entered her in one smooth stroke.

I heard her gasp and removed my hand. I looked down into her heavy-lidded eyes as I pulled out and then back in as I slowly increased the pace. I reached down, threading my fingers through hers as I rode her, claiming her. It felt right.

We fell asleep together on that small bed, tangled in each other's arms. Sometime during the night, I woke up and pulled her on top of me. Her eyes wide as she stared down at me. I helped her lower herself onto my hard length.

She took me. All of me. Like we were made for each other, I grabbed her hips as she began to rock. Soon, we were both gasping for breath. As I worked her breasts, she threw back her head, her lengthy hair flowing down her back. When we both came, she slumped against me, and I held her pressed into my chest, still connected. I rolled so we were both on our side and then we fell asleep again, our sweat-drenched bodies sticking to each other.

I blinked my eyes open to find her watching me as she lay beside me, an unreadable look on her face. It made me uncomfortable.

"Carson—"

I cut her off again, "Anna, whatever you have to tell me can wait until after we shower. Tell me over breakfast."

She closed her eyes in defeat and nodded, "Alright, Carson." I jumped up and held out my hand as I turned on the cabin shower. We barely fit in the small space, but we soaped and caressed each other thoroughly. I knew I was putting off the inevitable. I had a feeling I wouldn't like whatever she had to tell me. I wasn't even worried about what it could be. I arrogantly thought whatever it was, I would fix it.

Once we were dry, I got dressed in my clothes, and she put on shorts and a cute top. Her dark hair was damp from the shower. "Breakfast first? Then we can come back here to talk."

I watched as she bit her lip and nodded. We walked out of her cabin and turned to see one of the cruise line's staff, dressed all in white, approaching us. He carried a note in his hand. His face was expressionless as he looked from Anna to me.

"Mrs. Graham Johnson?" Anna turned white as she silently nodded. "I'm here to notify you that your husband's been taken to the hospital. There's a car waiting for you now. We've already docked, so you'll be allowed to depart early."

"Thank you. It'll only take me a minute to pack my things."

As the man turned away, I stood there shocked, in stunned disbelief. "You're married?"

She turned to me, guilt clouding her eyes, "Yes. I tried to tell you. I can explain—"

"What the fuck, Anna? You tried to tell me? That is something you should have told me immediately. That first night before I kissed you." I swing away from her, furious, only to turn back, shaking with my pent-up rage. "You cheated on your husband—"

She looked up at me, her stricken face showing her remorse; her lips trembled as she tried to hold back a sob, "No. It's not like that. Carson, you don't understand. Graham, he's—"

"What's there to understand, Anna?" My voice cut through the air, sharp with anger. "You pledged yourself to another

man. And then you let me... How could you let me do that?"
Shame burned in my gut as my heart ached. "I'm not a cheater.
Not like you." My lip curled as I looked at her, the words
dripping with scorn.

Her cheeks glistened from her tears. "Carson, right now, I
need to get to the hospital. But I'll call you later, I'll explain
about—"

I viciously cut her off. "No. I don't want you to call me. I don't
want to see or hear from you ever again." Fury choked my
voice. In a low, deadly tone, I told her, "You lied by omission,
Anna. You're dead to me."

With that, I turned and walked away, each step echoing the
finality of my words. I pretended not to hear the strangled
sob that ripped through the silence, a sound that hammered
a painful echo in my chest.

Six

Anna

I blink my eyes open. Immediately, I'm wide awake when I spot Carson sitting across from me. His face like granite, his hands clenched at his sides. I wearily sit up, rubbing my eyes. I lift my chin slightly at the look in his eyes as I try to calm my breathing.

I lick my dry lips as the silence stretches across the room, thick with unspoken emotions and past hurts, and I feel again the sting of his disapproval.

I twist my lips in a grimace. I should have known he wouldn't make this easy for me. And why should he? He obviously thinks the worst. I square my shoulders and clear my throat.

Finally, I begin to talk in a low voice, "When I found out I was pregnant with your child. I... I tried to call you. But you had blocked my calls."

I watch as he slowly crosses his arms over his chest, "If you truly wanted to contact me, you'd have found a way," his voice tight, his eyes unreadable.

"Yes, you're right. But knowing what you thought of me after what happened...," I glance over at him, then away, "And probably still think—. I decided it was best for me and Connor if you never found out you had a son."

"Obviously, you were wrong. It's apparent that what you thought was best wasn't." His words and eyes like steel, he continues in a tight voice, "Otherwise, Connor wouldn't have secretly skipped school and hopped on a bus - alone to try and find me."

I feel my cheeks burn under his unwavering gaze, "I didn't realize how badly Connor wanted to learn about his father. It wasn't..." My voice trails off, searching for an excuse, but

I can't find one. I twist my fingers together. "I should have known once he found that picture of us…"

Carson nods, "Yes, he looks just like I did when I was his age." I notice the glint of pride in his eyes as he talks about Connor. "I might have even hopped a bus or two. He's gutsy I'll give him that. What bothers me is what could have happened if I hadn't been at the office." He looks over at me, and I can see the accusation in his eyes.

"Yes, that bothers me, too." I glance back at Carson and take a deep breath. "Now that you know about Connor. I.. um… I suppose you'll want to spend some time with him?"

"Spend some time with him?" His voice echoes in the room, each word a hammer blow to my already fragile hope. He shoots up from the chair and starts pacing in front of me.

He spins around, towering over me. "Yes, Anna. I want to spend some time with my son. I think it's only fair since you've had him all to yourself for ten years."

The knot of fear in my stomach tightens. I knew this conversation was coming, but the possessiveness in his tone cuts deep.

"We just moved to Orlando. My lease is temporary. I would be willing to move closer—" I stop mid-sentence as Carson shakes his head slowly, a gesture that sends a fresh wave of panic through me. What's he planning? What does he want?

I try again. "Moving closer isn't an option? Fine. If you'd rather just see him during summer vacation—" Again, he shakes his head, his face expressionless.

I narrow my eyes at him, the feeling of being trapped in a predator's gaze intensifying. "What do you want, Carson?" I ask flatly.

He meets my gaze head-on. A cold smile plays on his lips. "I want my son to live with me. Full time."

I jump to my feet so quickly that I sway, the breath catching in my throat. I turn to look at Carson. "No, you can't take my son. He doesn't even know you! I'm his mother, the only parent he's ever known."

Carson just gives me a hard smile, a glint of steel in his eyes. "He's also my son. And the only reason he doesn't know me is because you kept his existence a secret." He calmly glances down at his Rolex and then back at me as if discussing the time and not threatening to rip my world apart.

"Carson, I know you can't forgive me. But you can't take Connor away." I look up at him with an earnest expression,

"Think of your son. You'd be hurting him. This isn't you, Carson. You're better than this."

He rears his head back at my words, "Don't presume that you know me, Anna. Eleven years is a long time. And I am considering my son. He came here to find me. He reached out to me. I'm sure a judge would take that under consideration..."

I feel helpless as my world seems to crumble around me. I feel like Carson's enjoying his little cat-and-mouse game with me. I decide not to play along. I turn my back on him, walk over to the sofa and sit down.

I glance back at him over my shoulder, "You can try, Carson. I may not be as wealthy as you are, but I have resources. My husband left me a wealthy widow. If I have to fight this in court, I will."

I notice his eyes turn to slits at the reminder of my late husband, but I don't care. I won't let him take away my son. "I'll do whatever it takes to remain in my son's life," I state with a tilt of my chin, determination evident in every line of my body.

At his silence, I look up to see that he's giving me a considering look.

"Whatever it takes, Anna?" He asks smoothly.

I frown up at him, "Yes, Carson, I will not give up my son."

"Alright, then here's my offer," Carson declares, his voice containing a dangerous edge. "I want Connor with me. If you insist on being a part of his life, you're welcome to move in with us."

Heat colors my cheeks, mirroring the flare of anger in my eyes. This cannot be happening. Ten years, I've built a life with my son. A life I thought was secure. Yet, now, it's being torn apart, and Carson seems to revel in his control over me. Panic builds inside me, but I force it down. I won't let him see my fear.

"It's an absurd proposal, a slap in the face disguised as a sympathetic offer," I scoff, "It's insane, Carson. Why would you even consider that?" I glare at him, "You can barely stand to look at me, let alone have me living under the same roof as you!"

"That's beside the point, Anna. You make a valid argument. I wouldn't want Connor to suffer by taking away his mother."

He glances over at me with a casual shrug, "However, it's up to you. You can take it or leave it." With those parting words, Carson nods cooly, turns, and leaves the room, leaving me trembling with the unfairness of it all. He's acting like my judge and jury all over again.

He wouldn't let me explain; he doesn't know the facts. He walked away eleven years ago with the same stubbornness he shows today. I should hate him for his arrogance, his judgment, and his absolute refusal to listen. It's easier for him to think the worst of me.

I should hate him… but I don't. I feel a pang of longing shoot through me as I remember the Carson I spent time with on the ship. He was… kind and thoughtful. His easygoing demeanor was very different from the man standing before me moments ago. The old Carson was willing to listen when I talked. That Carson was attracted to me, desired me. But that was before I hurt him.

He feels I betrayed him as well as my husband. There was a time when I would have shared the details of my marriage with Carson. Back then, I believe he would have understood, and he would have forgiven me. But he was stubborn and so full of self-righteousness. He could only see my actions in black and white, with no room for the gray areas that made up my life, my choices.

And now, he's trying to take my son away from me. He doesn't deserve to know the truth! Suddenly, the guilt hits me; like a wave, it washes away my anger. What I just thought is not entirely true… He even admitted, albeit arrogantly, that he didn't want to hurt Connor by forcing us apart. That's why he offered for me to move in with them. He and I both know I don't have a choice. If I want to be near my son, I will have to move in with Carson.

That thought tightens the knot that's already formed in my stomach. Living under the same roof with a man I resent and... still yearn for? This is a nightmare come true.

Seven

Carson

When I open my eyes, the first thing I'm aware of is the aroma of freshly brewed coffee. When I emerge from my bedroom, I'm dressed in brown cargo shorts and a blue polo shirt. I head straight to the kitchen as the delicious smell of sizzling bacon mingles with the scent of coffee.

I stop short when I see Anna standing in front of the stove. She has on white shorts and a white and blue halter top that shows off her tanned back. She's barefoot with a kitchen towel tied around her waist as an apron. She's flipping a perfectly browned pancake as I saunter up to the coffee pot. I pour myself a cup of coffee as my eyes search the apartment.

I hear Anna give a soft laugh, "If you're looking for Connor, good luck. He can be extremely hard to get up in the mornings," she says over her shoulder. "But I've found that bacon works better than any alarm clock."

As she continues to cook a pile of pancakes, I get out plates and silverware and set the dining room table. I place butter on the table and look around for the syrup we bought, but can't find it.

I hear the spare bedroom door open and out comes a rumpled Connor, still in his shorts and T-shirt that he slept in. He mumbles something that resembles a good morning but then disappears in the direction of the bathroom.

Anna brings the food to the table. I automatically reach to help her with the pancakes and bacon, and I can tell by her startled expression that she's not used to getting assistance.

She deftly places the stack of golden pancakes on the table. I set down the plate of crispy bacon, as she goes over to the microwave and gets out the syrup. I smile, as they're nothing better than hot syrup on pancakes. I notice she also fried three eggs, and she put the smaller plate down near the head of the table.

Right about then, Connor comes out of the bathroom, looking slightly less rumpled. It looks like he half-heartedly attempted to brush his hair, as it still sticks up in the back. He pulls out a chair and slumps into it, still half asleep.

I take a seat at the head of the table while Anna pours a large glass of milk for Connor, setting it down beside him. He picks it up and takes a long gulp before he mumbles a belated, "Thanks, Mom."

Anna just smiles. I watch as Connor reaches for the pile of pancakes. He spears four at once, transferring them to his plate with ease. Then he smears them with butter and drowns them in the warm syrup.

I help myself to three pancakes, and they pass the plate to Anna. I do the same with the bacon. After she takes a few slices, she whispers, "You might want to take a bit more because Connor typically eats anything that isn't already taken."

I chuckle as I take a few more slices of bacon. Sure enough, I watch as Connor makes short work of his four pancakes and the remaining bacon. I grin over at Anna, "I see what you mean. He's a bottomless pit disguised as a boy." Her answering smile is swift, and we share a smile of amusement between us. Connor pretends he doesn't hear us and continues to focus on shoveling in his food.

Once all the plates are empty, Anna gets up and silently warms up her coffee and mine. Connor finally glances up from his plate as he finishes off his glass of milk.

He looks from me to Anna with raised eyebrows, "What are we doing today?"

I look from him to his mother. "What would you like to do?" As I try to think of places a ten-year-old would like to visit, "There's the zoo, or we could go to the beach."

Connor turns around with wide eyes, "I want to go to the zoo. We had beaches in Lauderdale."

I look at Anna, who smiles, her eyes lighting up, "I haven't been to a zoo in ages. It sounds like fun."

I help Anna clear the table, and while she's loading the dishes in the dishwasher, I give Suzanne, my admin, a call.

"Hi, Carson. I've rescheduled all of your meetings for next week and the week after. Your schedule is cleared," replies my always efficient administrative assistant.

"Great. Thanks. I'll be in next Monday."

"Carson, if anyone asked, I told them you had something come up at the last minute."

"Thank you. You can tell my brothers the same thing if they ask. I'll be sure to talk to them myself before Monday."

"Perfect. Enjoy your time off, Carson."

"I will."

I look up as Connor steps out of the bedroom in shorts and a T-shirt. He has a baseball hat on his head.

"Alright, let's go," I announce as I rub my hands in front of me and hold open the door.

When we enter the grounds of the Jacksonville Zoo and Gardens, Connor is practically bouncing with excitement as he runs ahead of us.

"Don't get too far ahead, Connor," Anna calls after him.

The day is bright with sunshine and the sky is a clear azure blue with hardly a cloud in the sky.

Anna glances over a me and says, "We couldn't have picked a better day."

I grin in agreement as I pull out the provided map of the animal exhibits. We briefly skim the brochure and then put it away as we follow the main trail that leads us to the African Loop.

It's a long boardwalk where we can observe the animals in an open environment.

We see the flamingos first. Anna walks over to the plaque and reads, "Flamingos get their pink color from the carotenoid pigments they get from the shrimp and algae they eat."

Connor turns to us and says, "They must eat a lot of shrimp to get that pink." Then he laughs as if he told a joke.

His steps fly over the boardwalk as we continue walking the loop. He sees a warthog and starts singing a song from the movie The Lion King. Then he stops singing, and his eyes go wide when he spies the zoo's white rhinoceros.

"He's huge. I've never seen a rhinoceros before," he admits. "The white ones are rare," I tell him as I read the plaque. He just nods at my words, not taking his eyes off the beast.

Connor loves the zebras. Anna and I both are snapping photos as we meander along while Connor sprints from one exhibit to the other. "Connor, stand over here so I can get the zebras in the background." Connor faces her with a big grin on his face, and then he's off again, practically running toward the next exhibit.

We spend extra time when we reach the Elephant Plaza. Since the day is hot, the behemoth animals loiter in the shallow pool as their trunks spray water onto their backs.

Next up is the Giraffe Overlook. Connor practically vibrates with excitement as we climb the stairs to a wide desk that puts us at eye level with the lofty animals. Their long necks sway gracefully, and their gentle eyes follow us around.

Connor erupts with an excited giggle as one of the creatures reaches in and nibbles the twig he holds out to it. "Did you see? Did you see the giraffe eat it right out of my hand?" he asks, his voice high-pitched with joy.

Anna and I both give him a fond smile as his mother says, "Yes, I snapped a picture," she states, showing him the image on her phone.

"Cool!" Connor declares before bounding off again.

An older couple standing nearby sees Anna taking pictures, "Would you like us to take a picture of your family in front of the giraffes?"

I see Anna's cheeks go pink, but none of us feel the need to correct the woman. Instead, we simply line up in front of the majestic animals, turn, and smile at the lady. I place my hand on Connor's shoulder as the woman takes a couple of photos.

Before we walk down from the platform, I check my phone. I already have half a dozen pictures of my son. Each photo captures a different image of his youthful, wide-eyed wonder. I suspect images of him will soon be filling up my phone, like all the other proud parents I know.

I glance up and see Anna giving me a knowing look. I immediately give her a crooked smile back, forgetting in the moment my harsh animosity toward her.

Connor yells, "Mom! Mom! Look at the tigers!" My eyes follow Anna as she hurries to catch up with our son. I notice how the sunlight brings out the highlights in her chestnut hair. The sway of her hips and her long, shapely legs. I hear her laugh at something Connor says, and the soft chime of her laughter reminds me of how much I enjoyed spending time with her before—

"Dad!" The single word bursts from Connor; it is just one word, but it freezes me in place. I glance up to see Connor gesturing wildly for me to join them. My throat tightens with pent-up emotions. He probably doesn't even realize that's the first time he's ever called me that. It just came tumbling out naturally in his eagerness to get my attention. It's a slip of the tongue for him, but it feels like a dam has broken within me.

It releases a flood of emotions that threatens to overflow as I quickly brush the back of my hand over my eyes.

As I approach, I glance over Connor's head and see Anna, suspicious moisture in her eyes. She tries unsuccessfully to blink it away. She gives me a watery smile and just nods. It's a sweet moment of unspoken understanding shared between us. Our son is blissfully oblivious to the emotions swirling around him. He continues to exclaim over the shaggy, powerful beasts pacing back and forth in their large enclosure.

We stop for lunch within the zoo at the Palm Plaza Cafe. After we get our sandwiches, we find a table shaded from the bright sun and sit down. Connor can hardly sit still in his seat as he describes the different animals he's seen so far.

I sit there amidst the sights and sounds of the zoo. The murmur of the crowd of people around us and Connor's animated face as he mimics an elephant lifting his trunk. I realize that I haven't felt this happy, this content in a long time. My eyes go to Connor and the woman sitting beside him. Her chin propped on her hand as she smiles at our son. She reaches out and gently smooths a stray lock from his forehead. I witness the love she feels for him, and something shifts inside me. She's suddenly the same girl I fell for all those years ago.

I have to remind myself of her betrayal. I need to keep that at the forefront. She's a danger to my equilibrium, and I need to keep my distance.

I abruptly stand. "Let me throw these containers away," I say gruffly as I pick them up and find a trash can.

By the time I feel in control and walk back, Connor is up on his feet and practically dragging Anna toward the next exhibit. Luckily, it's another large cat breed, a shadow of jaguars. Connor immediately falls silent as he studies them. They flick their tails lazily back and forth, yet their gazes remain alert and intense, betraying them as predators.

I read the plaque, "Shadow of Jaguars. Jaguars are solitary animals and don't usually form groups. They are sometimes called a 'prowl' or a 'leap,' but the term 'shadow' emphasizes their ability to blend into their surroundings."

I turn to look at my son, and he seems fascinated with the large cats, "You know we have a football team here, the Jacksonville Jaguars. We'll have to go to a game sometime."

He blinks up at me then a grin spreads across his face. "Cool." I smile down at him and resist the urge to ruffle his hair.

After snapping more photos with Connor in front of the spotted cats, we continue on our way.

"Dad, what's next?" He asks me.

"River Valley Aviary," as he cocks his head with a confused frown, "Birds," I clarify.

"Oh... neat," then he's running ahead again and urging us to follow him.

"I wish I had his energy," I say ruefully to Anna.

She grins and shakes her head. "If we could only bottle it!" With her eyes on Connor ahead of us, she says, "You know, most of the time, he acts like he's ten going on thirty. I like seeing him being a normal, carefree child again."

Right then, Connor turns back and yells, "I hear them. The birds! Hurry!"

Eight

Anna

I look in the back seat and see Connor passed out. The only thing keeping him upright is his seatbelt. I turn back to the front with a soft smile on my face.

Carson glances over at me and then looks in the rearview mirror. I see the grin spread across his face as he says in a low voice, "This is the first time today he's been still. I see he finally ran out of steam." I see the fondness for our son in his eyes.

"Yes," I nod, then hesitantly turn toward Carson in my seat. "Thank you for today. Connor really enjoyed himself. The zoo was the perfect outing."

Carson keeps his eyes on the road as he nods in response to my words. "I enjoyed it, too." He admits with a grin. "You've done a good job raising him, Anna. It shows."

A wide smile blooms on my face because I know that was hard for him to admit. "Thank you. I like to think so." As I turn forward in my seat, I continue. "When do you want us to move in?"

His eyes quickly slant my way, "That depends on how quickly you can settle things in Orlando. I'm not sure what transferring his school records involves…"

"We just had them transferred to Orlando, so I can request they forward them on. I can contact the school district tomorrow and start the process. His grades shouldn't suffer if he misses a few more days. He's a good student."

"And your place in Orlando?"

I sigh with frustration, "Well, I'm on a temporary month-to-month lease because the sale of the house I wanted fell through. Everything that could have gone wrong did. Most of our possessions are still in moving boxes."

"Why don't you just have the moving company pick everything up and have it delivered here."

I consider his suggestion, "That's not a bad idea. I had ordered some basic furniture, but the delivery was delayed. I should be able to cancel the order." I turn back to him, "I'll do that. I'll call them as well and ask if they can deliver our boxes to your place."

I take a deep breath, willing the nervous flutter in my stomach to calm. "Carson, since I'm staying," I begin, my voice firm. The words "not that I had much choice" flicker through my mind, but I bite them back. A smile, more hopeful than genuine, stretches across my face. "If we want Connor to feel secure, you'll have to stop treating me like the enemy."

I glance at him to see his jaw tight, and his eyes narrowed on the road. He doesn't even glance my way. But at least he appears to be mulling things over. I give him that time. The ride to his apartment stretches on, the silence tense.

Once Carson pulls into the parking garage, Connor blinks, then rubs the sleep out of his eyes. "We're home?"

"Yeah, Buddy," Carson says with a smile and a look in the rearview mirror.

The elevator ride is mostly silent as Connor isn't fully awake yet. But the moment we step into the apartment, he looks around and declares, "When's dinner?"

I give a light laugh, "I'm not sure what your dad has on hand. I'll do some grocery shopping tomorrow, though."

We both turn and look at Carson, who seems at a loss, "There are plenty of restaurants around…"

I gently interject, "We could order a pizza."

Connor's face lights up. "Yeah, pizza would be great. Can we get pepperoni?"

Carson looks at Connor's hopeful eyes, "Sure, why not? Pizza for dinner tonight."

I hide a grin and add, "I like anything. Except anchovies."

Carson grins back. "I'll order two pizzas. One pepperoni and one with meat and vegetables."

He pulls out his phone and calls in the order, "One small pepperoni. No, wait. Make that a medium pepperoni and a large Super Supreme…"

I look at Connor, "Why don't you take a shower while we wait for the pizza?"

Connor mumbles an agreement and heads down the hallway.

A few minutes later, Carson and Connor both join me at the table, looking freshly showered, hair damp but combed.

Right on cue, the doorbell rings, and Carson gets the pizza and brings it to the table.

"Connor quickly grabs a slice of gooey cheese and pepperoni and takes a huge bite. "I love pizza," he says with his mouth half full. I give him a warning look, which he ignores with a grin and finishes chewing.

"Sorry," he mumbles before taking another giant bite.

Carson opens the second box, and I take a slice while Carson grabs two slices. The only sounds are the satisfying crunch as we all enjoy the hot, cheesy pizzas in front of us.

Finally, with three slices in his stomach, Connor breaks the silence.

"What are we doing tomorrow?" He asks with wide, expectant eyes as he looks at Carson.

I bite my lips with a grin as I glance down at my plate without lifting my eyes. I feel Carson glance at me for help, but I keep my eyes downcast.

"Um, I'm not sure. I'm still thinking it over." He leans forward and asks Connor, "What do you normally do for fun?"

Connor answers quickly, "I like to ride my bike. Jeff and I used to play basketball, but he's in Lauderdale. I like video games and music. Some movies, but not the boring ones Mom likes to watch. I normally have practice after school." He shrugs.

"What sports are you interested in?" Carson asks, genuinely curious.

Connor's eyes light up, "I like track and basketball mainly. I like to run. I'm fast. That's something I can do by myself. Basketball, I can practice by myself, but it's funner with more people."

"More fun," I automatically correct him.

"Yeah, it's more fun with a team or Jeff..." he looks over at Carson with a bit of longing in his eyes.

Carson immediately says, "I like to play basketball. We can do a little one-on-one tomorrow."

Connor's eyes go wide, and he grins, "Cool." Then he gives a small frown, "Can I meet my grandma?" Suddenly, he looks uncertain.

I quickly glance at Carson, but he must have seen the vulnerability in our son's eyes as he says with utter confidence, "Of course. She'll insist on seeing you." He leans forward as if telling my son a secret. "I selfishly didn't want to share you with my family yet. You can meet her tomorrow."

Connor's cheeks get rosy, and his eyes go wide; he looks down with a sheepish grin, "Yeah, it would be really cool to meet my grandma."

"I'll clear the table; you guys go check out what's streaming on TV."

As I put the dishes in the dishwasher and wrap up any leftovers, I listen to them both discuss the merits of what's available to watch. They have similar tastes, and I shrug, refusing to be offended that they don't like the Hallmark channel or Rom-Coms. It's a male thing. At least I can still read romance books on my e-reader if I'm going to be now surrounded by so much testosterone.

A pang of jealousy shoots through me as I listen to them bond. I quickly tamp it down, reminding myself that this is what's best for Connor. But I still feel the sharp tug in my heart at having to share my son with someone else. Even if that person is his father and has every right to be a part of Connor's life, it still causes an unfamiliar ache.

My hand hesitates as I hit the cycle button on the dishwasher. I hear the chugging of the motor and the swish of the water. My life is changing, morphing into something unfamiliar. The loneliness I've grown accustomed to feels different now, sharper somehow.

I blink away sentimental tears as a part of me wonders, 'What about me'? I'll be left living a second-hand life with a man who's only interested in having me around for his son. Will it make a difference even if he agrees to call a truce? I doubt it. Carson's been carrying the weight of what he thinks is my betrayal for far too many years.

He thinks it's my fault, and it is. I should have immediately told him I was married and the circumstances of my marriage in name only. But I was too busy wearing rose-colored glasses and falling head over heels in love.

Oh, yes, I fell in love with Carson on that cruise. Why else would I have slept with him? He thinks I betrayed my wedding vows, but I know I didn't. I lift my chin.

I remember the frantic ride to the hospital. Graham was so sick when I arrived. It wasn't until three days later that he was coherent enough to sense that something was off with me.

He was so kind; even as weak as he was, he knew I was hurting.

When he asked me what happened on the cruise, I was hesitant to tell him. I knew he'd insist that I leave him and go after Carson. 'Follow your heart,' he would have advised me. But I couldn't do that to Graham. He had no one else. No one to care for him. He was so weak those last few years. Ultimately, I had to hire someone to help me lift him, and even then, it was hard. So hard. My heart aches for how the illness devastated his body.

Dear kind-hearted Graham. I blink away my tears. I miss him; he was such a good person. He didn't deserve to die the way he did. Nobody does.

"Mom?" My son's voice stringent voice penetrates the fog of memories.

I look up, startled to see two pairs of eyes looking at me expectantly. I feel the blush as it covers my cheeks, "Sorry, I missed what you said."

My son gets a slight look of concern, "That's okay." He turns toward Carson, "She sometimes misses Graham," he explains with a preteen shrug. Not recognizing the instant tension in the room as Carson's face turns harsh. An unreadable expression crosses his face as his cold eyes meet mine.

Carson abruptly turns away, leaving Connor to ask again. "Do you want to watch Galaxy Quest or Jimungi?"

"Really? You even have to ask?" I say, a teasing note in my voice.

My son heaves a heavy sigh filled with disappointment as he turns around and tells Carson, "I told you she'd pick Galaxy Quest. It's one of her favorites."

I hear Carson say as I step into the living room, "That's fine, we'll watch Jumanji tomorrow." He promises Connor with a wink.

As Carson brings up the movie, Connor looks over a me, "Can we have popcorn?"

"Connor, you just finished dinner. Aren't you still full from the pizza?"

"But Mom, we're watching a movie," he whines as he gives me a look as if I'm depriving him of sustenance. "We always have popcorn when we watch a movie."

I glance at Carson, hoping for backup, but he only lifts his eyebrows and says, "I have microwave popcorn."

"Fine, I'm obviously outnumbered," I mutter as I mock frown and go back into the kitchen. Carson yells, "It's in the cabinet above the refrigerator." I stand, looking up at the cabinet, then I look around for a step stool.

I walk back into the living room, "I can't reach the cabinet, and there's no step stool." I say simply.

Carson's eyes roam over me without comment, and he strides into the kitchen. When I walk in behind him, he's pulled down two boxes of popcorn. "We'll have to find a different place for these."

He opens another tall cabinet and retrieves two bowls from the top shelf that look perfect for popcorn and hands them to me. Before he heads back to the living room, he grabs a cold beer for himself and a root beer for Connor. He places a root beer on the counter for me, then leaves me to fix the popcorn. I give a secret smile. He remembered I like root beer.

Nine

Carson

The bedside lamp casts long shadows on the wall as I again stay by Connor's bedside while he falls asleep.

I try to shake off my mixed feelings. I'm not used to the emotional roller coaster I've been on since Connor stepped into my life. My lips twist in a self-deprecating grimace. Not just Connor but Anna as well.

When she didn't answer Connor's call, he raced into the kitchen to ask her. When she looked up with tears glistening in her eyes, I felt a powerful urge to comfort her. The feeling coursed through me, but years of self-preservation held me back. She looked like she was hurting, and I couldn't believe how much I wanted to soothe away her pain.

Then, when Connor so casually explained she was missing Graham, his words cut through me like a sharp knife. Graham. Her ex-husband is the constant elephant in the room. A silent ghost who will always stand between us. A barrier that I almost welcome, as I don't want to let down my defenses when I'm around her.

However, she's right that we need to call a truce for Connor's sake. My son is my number one priority right now. My eyes rove over him again as I feel what is now becoming a familiar tightening in my chest.

I lean down and adjust the covers. I owe it to my son to try and make peace with his mother. And I smile as I think of my mother. My lips turn up into a wide smile as I imagine her reaction once she hears the news of her grandson.

I have to tell my brothers as well. It was the truth that I wanted to keep Connor's existence to myself for a while. All these emotions are like a battering ram, shoving me one way then another. These past few days - a far cry from my orderly routines.

I give a silent laugh as I close Connor's bedroom door. Even with all the chaos, I feel like there's a newfound purpose in my life—a new beginning.

I sober as I stride into the living room. When I see Anna sitting on the couch, I know she stayed up waiting for me. Then, the air is thick with tension as I sit in the armchair across from her.

"Connor is very important to me." I say in a resigned voice, "So, I think a truce between us, while it won't be easy, is necessary."

I watch as she leans forward, her hands clasped before her. A look of relief flashes across her face. "Thank you."

"Now, I have a few questions," I warn her firmly. Her eyes warily meet mine, but she doesn't protest. "I want my son to have my last name. Who is listed as the father on his birth certificate?"

"I understand," Anna finally manages. I watch as she licks her lips, a nervous habit. Avoiding my eyes, she reluctantly answers, "His birth certificate doesn't list a father. It's blank."

I narrow my eyes at her as I clarify. "We don't need to remove Graham's name?" My voice sounds tight and tinged with doubt.

"No. Like I said, I left it blank." She lifts her eyes to mine, an unreadable look in them.

"What's Connor's full name? He goes by Johnson, right?"

She nods and states quietly, "Yes. It was easier since that was my last name. His full name is Connor Carlton Johnson." When I suck in my breath sharply at his middle name, she looks up at me with a soft smile. "I remember you mentioned your father once, and you said his name was Carlton. So, I... I gave him that as a middle name."

"You named him after my father?" I say in stunned disbelief.

"Yes." She doesn't elaborate, but her eyes give me a soulful look.

I clamp my teeth tightly together because there are so many questions I want to ask her. Questions about her husband and her marriage. Did he think Connor was his? Didn't he question when she didn't list him as the father?

But there's a bigger part of me that doesn't want to know the answers. I don't want to even think of her with another man. I blink. Shouldn't I be more worried that this man helped raise my son, at least for the first three or four years of his life? I need to focus on my son, not his mother or what type of marriage she had. But the questions still linger. Making me wonder...

I pull my thoughts away and look over at Anna as I clear my throat.

"I'll get with my lawyer to have the paperwork updated," I finish vaguely.

She just nods, her clear gray eyes studying my face as she says, "You'll probably want a paternity test."

I remain motionless for a beat, and then I nod, "Yes, but only to make it official. I'm convinced he's mine."

I meant the words to reassure her, but I see twin flags of color mark her cheeks as if my words offend her, but she presses her lips together without saying another word.

I watch her for another moment or two, but it seems she's learning to hide her emotions. Yet her eyes are so expressive, I remember getting lost in those deep, clear pools.

I clear my throat again. "It sounds like we have a lot of paperwork to get started. If you need my lawyer to help with the school records, let me know." I stand, and without a backward glance, I leave her sitting there, alone on the couch.

Once I'm in bed, I can't forget the look she gave me after she shared that our son was named after my father. I remember mentioning my parents to her and telling her how close-knit my family was. I blinked again to try and dislodge the wounded deer look she gave me as if it hurt her that I wasn't there with her to name our child.

The walls feel like they're closing in on me as I lie in bed, trying to slow my racing heartbeat. Sleep is hard to find, and as I toss and turn, images of our time together repeat in my mind. So does Anna's easy smile, the sound of her laughter, the way we communicated with just a glance.

How compatible we were. Inside and outside of bed. I roll over and viciously punch my pillow, turning it over and searching for a cooler spot for my heavy head. Sometime in the wee hours, I finally fall into a restless sleep.

When I climb out of bed the next morning, I'm surprised to see it's after nine. I listen, but I don't hear any sounds coming from the rest of the apartment. I throw on a pair of boxers and tentatively open my bedroom door. I'm alone in the apartment.

For one split second, panic freezes my limbs as I imagine she's left and taken my son with her. Alarm flares through me, followed quickly by a surge of pure disbelief. I walk furiously through the empty living room as the silence presses in on me. Then I see a note on the dining room table. I pick it up, *'Gone to get groceries. Connor is with me. Be back later. Anna'.*

I take a deep, calming breath as a wave of relief washes over me. Yet, I still detour into her and Connor's rooms just to confirm their clothes and things are still there. I even glance into the main bathroom and give a rueful grin when I spot their toothbrushes. Maybe I'm overreacting.

After I dress in blue jeans and a golf shirt, I pick up my phone and give my mother a call. "Hey, Mom, do you have any plans for today?"

Later, when I hear Anna and Connor at the door, I open it and swing it wide. I reach out to help take some of the bags.

"There's more in the car," Anna says with a slight smile. "I hope you don't mind. I like to cook, so I got enough to last through the week. Kind of. It's hard to tell with a growing boy." She says as she throws a grin at Connor. Then she looks back at me, "Did you eat breakfast? Connor and I had cereal."

"That's what I ate too." She arches her brows in surprise and gives me a playful look, "How long has it been since you last had a bowl of cereal?" She asks me.

"About twenty years ago or so." I shrug as I admit that and follow her to the garage to get the rest of the groceries. As we come back up, we continue the conversation. "So, which crunch cereal did you have?"

I turn and give her a serious look, "Cap'n Crunch. It is the best." I say tongue in cheek.

"Of course." We share a grin.

As I set the bags on the kitchen counter, I feel some of the tension between us ease. Maybe this truce thing isn't so bad. Then Anna starts to put the groceries away. I feel a wave of heat travel through me as she reaches overhead. Her shirt rides up, leaving a sliver of bare skin exposed. Just that glimpse of her taunt mid-drift has me wanting to reach out and run my hand along her smooth skin.

I have to drag my eyes away, and then a twinge of resentment floods through me. It's not her fault, I remind myself. But the unwanted reaction frustrates me.

Connor comes into the kitchen right then. He's already reaching for a snack.

"I thought I'd drive us over to see my mother. She's expecting us for lunch."

A wide grin practically splits Connor's face. "Great. When can we leave?"

I laugh, "Anytime. I know she won't mind if we're early."

Connor looks over at his mother, "Mom, can we leave now?"

Anna smiles and says, "Sure, but why don't you wash up and brush your hair while I put these last few items away?"

For the first time since I've known my son, he seems concerned with his appearance. He abruptly turns and practically runs to the bathroom to slick down his hair. When he emerges, his hair is neatly combed, and his face is shiny from scrubbing it with a washcloth.

Anna states, "Let me run a brush through my hair, and I'll be ready to go."

Connor prances from one foot to the other as we wait. The minute Anna reappears, he opens the front door. Once we get in the car, he says in a worried voice, "Should I have a gift or something for her?"

I meet his eyes in the rearview mirror, "No, Son. You'll be gift enough."

At my words, he seems to settle down and sits back. He perks up and looks around as I pull into the private drive that leads to my mother's river estate. Once I turn off the engine, Connor jumps out, but his steps slow as we move toward the door.

I come up behind him and place my hand on his shoulder. "My mom's name is Bonnie. But I'm sure she'll insist you call her grandma. She'll hug you for sure, and she might even mess up your hair." I warn him in a low voice.

I feel some of the tension ease from his shoulders. Then the door is opened by my mother. Her dark hair has a striking white streak that she brushes back from her forehead. She's an attractive woman, and the vivid blue of her eyes hasn't faded a bit.

She only has eyes for the young boy standing before her, and her eyes glow with instant love as she takes him in. "And you must be my grandson. Come here, young man, and let me love on you."

Connor steps forward, and she wraps her arms around him and pulls him into a warm and loving embrace. When she finally lets him up for air, his cheeks are rosy, and he doesn't even protest when she ruffles his combed hair, messing it up.

My mother's eyes are filled with joyous tears, and Connor's are suspiciously wet as he sniffles and wipes his eyes on the back of his sleeve.

With her arm tightening around Connor, pulling him closer, my mother turns to look at me and then Anna. Her eyes crinkle at the corners as she offers a welcoming smile to her grandson's mother. I see Anna's worried frown melt away, and my mom's smile widens, creating a warm exchange between them.

Anna's shoulders visibly relax, and she lets out a small breath she must have been holding. I feel a pang of guilt as I should have noticed Anna was more nervous than our son at meeting my mom. I reach out and place my hand, a gesture of reassurance, on the small of Anna's back. My eyes linger on the sway of her hips in her navy shorts as she proceeds me into my childhood home.

Ten

Anna

Carson's hand sends a shiver of awareness down my spine as we walk into his mother's spacious living room. The ceiling-to-floor windows are expansive, showing a breathtaking view of the St. John's River. It's a mix of decorating styles that is stylish and comfortable at the same time.

"Anna, please call me Bonnie. I've been looking forward to this visit." Bonnie leads Connor and me around the house while Carson disappears to the kitchen.

Bonnie looks down at Connor once she's given us a tour, "I just pulled some chocolate chip cookies out of the oven.

They're in the kitchen if you want one," she says with a fond smile. "I bet they're still warm."

Connor's eyes go wide with delight as he bounds into the kitchen ahead of us. "Grandma, I found the cookies," Connor yells. Bonnie gets a big smile on her face at hearing the word grandma fall from his lips.

"Here, let me get you a plate." She gives Carson a smile of approval when she sees he's already got a glass of milk ready for Connor. She slides two cookies on a plate for Connor and slides another plate of cookies between Carson and me.

I look around the spacious kitchen. It's white and bright and has all the latest appliances, yet still has a bit of country charm.

We all grin when Connor gives a contented sigh as the last bite of cookie disappears into his mouth. "Thanks, Grandma." He ignores the napkin I hold out and instead wipes his mouth with the back of his hand. He leaves a trace of chocolate on his chin.

In a voice filled with emotion, Carson asks, "So, Mom, what do you think of your grandson, Connor Carlton?"

"Connor Carlton?" Her eyes fly to Carson, and then she looks over at me. I smile and nod. "I named him after his grandfather."

When Carson's mother blinks, a single tear spills over onto her cheek. She gently wipes it away, her gaze lingering on me with a warmth that speaks volumes. Her eyes return to Connor as he finishes the last of his milk. "That's a very fine name," she says, her voice thick with emotion.

At lunchtime, we all sit down around her large dining room table. The aroma of Bonnie's huge tray of lasagna with garlic bread fills the air, making our mouths water. She has a grand time filling Connor's ear with funny stories about Carson and his brothers. My son's laughter is contagious, and soon, the dining room is filled with hearty laughter.

Afterward, we wander over the grounds. Bonnie's home sits on a huge piece of land directly on the St. John's River. She has a large boathouse that sits proudly by the dock. Connor is between Carson and me, each of us holding his hand. We stroll out over the wooden planks and perch on the edge, our feet dangling over the slow-moving river.

Dappled sunlight glints off the waves as we listen to the water lapping softly against the dock. The sound mingles with the chirping of birds overhead.

As we sit, I look over at my son, "Remember when we used to pick out images in the clouds?"

Connor scoffs, "When I was five."

I point to one of the cottony clouds overhead, "Doesn't that look like a duck?" He squints his eyes and says, "Yeah, and look at that one. That looks like an elephant."

Soon, Carson joins in. I have to pinch myself because it feels like we're a real family.

We reluctantly stand as the sun lowers in the sky and the shadows lengthen. We head back toward the house amid Connor's endless questions about the motorboat and going out on the water.

Connor is practically bouncing up and down when Carson promises we'll return for a boat ride. He explains the boat belongs to his brother. But Carter left the keys for any of the family to use.

"When can we go out on the boat?" Connor asks with wonder in his eyes. The eagerness in his voice tugs on my heartstrings.

Carson chuckles. "Thinking maybe tomorrow or the next day. Depends on when Uncle Chase wants us over for dinner. I'll call both my brothers tonight, but I have a feeling we'll be invited to come over tomorrow."

"Cool!" That one word conveys his eagerness to meet more of Carson's family.

"Connor, do you like to fish?" Carson asks.

"Fish? I don't know. I've never been fishing," Connor says, his eyes wide.

"We'll have to go fishing one day soon," Carson promises. Connor looks up at him with sincere eyes. "I think I'll like fishing with you, Dad."

Carson reaches out with one arm, unable to resist, and pulls our son into a side hug. "You bet you will," he says, his voice husky as he buries his face in Connor's soft hair.

I swallow the lump in my throat that's been there ever since we arrived. The entire day has been filled with emotional reunions between grandma and grandson, as well as a day of discovery between father and son. I've been trying to hold my emotions in check, otherwise I'll be crying uncontrollably and going through a box of tissues.

While the focus has been on our son, there's a subtle thread of awareness between his father and me. A few times today, I've turned and caught Carson's eyes lingering on me for a beat too long. His stares cause an unfamiliar heat to spread through my lower abdomen.

The more time we spend together, the easier the conversation flows between us. The way we seem to anticipate each other's thoughts - it's all so familiar. I thought those things had faded with time, but here they are, resurfacing.

Laughing at something Connor said, I look up to find Carson mirroring my amusement, shared laughter sparking in our eyes. Then, just as quickly, he looks away. A flicker of something akin to resentment crosses his features as if the reminder of our connection is unwelcome.

My smile falters. This unspoken tension between us, a tangled mess of emotions, adds another layer of complexity to our already strained relationship.

Soon, we're at the door saying our goodbyes to Bonnie. Connor snuggles closer to his grandma, clearly enjoying the newfound attention she's lavishing on him.

"You'll come back and visit me often, won't you?" she asks us. Carson smiles, "Yes, Mom. I was going to suggest that we throw a cookout, but later, after our immediate family gets to know everyone."

Bonnie smiles approvingly, "I think that sounds wonderful." She leans down so she's at eye level with Connor. "It was so wonderful to meet you, Connor. Knowing I have such a wonderful grandson makes me happy."

Connor ducks his head. "I like having a wonderful grandma, too." Carson's mother can't contain the smile that blooms across her face.

Later that night, we fall into what is becoming our nightly routine. I tuck Connor in and step out of the room, leaving Carson to say goodnight. He typically sits with Connor for a few minutes.

Tonight, when he comes out of Connor's room, he nods to me, "I'll see you and Connor in the morning. I'm going to call my brothers and let them know that I have a son. We'll probably be meeting at Chase's house tomorrow night."

"Alright. See you tomorrow," I say with a pasted-on smile.

After he turns and leaves the room, I go into the kitchen and pour myself a glass of white wine. I carry it with me into my bedroom. My gaze drifts around my room. It's fairly large, with a queen-sized bed, a large armchair, a mid-sized dresser, and a walk-in closet. It's decorated in all different colors of blue. It's beginning to feel like it's my space.

I put on my pajamas, a lightweight cotton cami, and short set. It has dainty scalloped piping around the edges that makes me feel feminine. I lounge in the armchair with my e-reader.

I sigh as I close the lid. I can't quite get into the story of the grumpy male character who falls head over heels for the heroine. Not when I have my very own version of an alpha grumpy male right down the hall.

And his hooded glances are doing a number on my dormant libido. At least it used to be dormant. I grin ruefully. Leaning my head back against the armchair, I close my eyes and think back over the afternoon and how it felt to sit on the dock like a real family.

It's what I used to dream about. Carson, me, and our son. Maybe if I had handled things differently or had explained about Graham, I grimace. The past is the past. And honestly, if I had to do things over - I still would have married Graham when he offered. I can't regret being there for him. No one should have to go through terminal cancer alone.

I wearily get up from the armchair and crawl into bed.

It feels like I have just closed my eyes when I hear my son cry out. I scramble to pull back the covers, jump out of bed, and rush to his bedside.

"Connor? Baby, you okay?" I approach the bed to find Connor with tears streaming down his face.

"Yeah," he sniffles. "I had a nightmare," he admits in a shaky voice. I sit down on the side of the bed, "You're safe." I reach out a hand and smooth his hair off his forehead. I reach down and place my hand on his shoulder. "Are you alright now?" I turn when I hear Carson at the door.

He has a frown on his face as he stands there in a pair of boxers and nothing else.

"I thought I heard something..." His voice trails off when he gets a good look at Connor's face. He comes over and crouches by Connor's bed. Close to where I'm already sitting, his bare torso brushes against my legs. "Hey, Buddy, you okay?"

Connor tries to wipe away his cheeks with a brave hiccup. "I had a nightmare. When I opened my eyes, it was black. I couldn't see anything."

Carson says, "Nightmares can be scary." He looks around and then over at the dark nightlight, "The bulb went out." He stands and runs a hand through his hair. "I think I may have another bulb or another night light. Let me check." He unplugs the light and takes it with him. He glances over at me with a nod, turns, and quietly leaves.

I reach out and take Connor's small hand in mine. "What was the nightmare about?" I ask gently.

"I dreamt that you and Dad left me," he sniffles again, "I was all alone."

I lean down and cradle him in my arms like when he was a baby. I rub his back as I lightly rock us back and forth, "You will never be alone, Connor. You have me and now your dad. We love you dearly, and we will never, ever leave you." He gives a shaky nod, still wrapped tightly in my arms.

"You even have a grandma. You saw how much she cares for you. Tomorrow, you'll meet even more family. And all of them will love you, too." I lean back and tilt his chin up. As I look into his watery eyes, a trace of fear still lingers. "You will never be alone. You will always be surrounded by family who love you. Understand?"

I watch as he smiles shakily, "Yeah, Mom. Thanks."

I reach out and cup his cheek. "I love you, kiddo. So, much. And so does your dad."

I'm suddenly aware of Carson's presence as he stands in the open doorway. He clears his throat as he steps into the room with a night light in his hand. He walks over to the wall opposite the bed and plugs it in. Instantly, the room is filled with dim light.

"There, that ought to do it. What do you think, Connor?" He asks solemnly.

Connor again sniffles and says, "Thanks, Dad."

"Anytime, Son." Carson walks over, leans down, and hugs him. "We're right down the hall if you need us. Got it?"

Finally, a sliver of a grin stretches across Connor's face, "Yeah. Both of you came."

"Yep. And we always will." He squeezes his shoulder and steps back. I lean in and place a gentle kiss on Connor's cheek. "Sleep tight, Baby."

He gives a huge yawn, rolls over, and hugs a pillow. I stand and join Carson at the door. He hesitates, and I say gently, "Let's leave the door open for tonight."

He gives a quick nod, abruptly turns, and walks hurriedly to his bedroom. I stand there watching his retreating backside. I shake my head with a frustrated shrug; what did I do this time to offend him? I swear there is no pleasing that man. With a sigh, I go back to my bed, crawl in, and resolutely shut my eyes, refusing to even dream about that man.

Eleven

Carson

My eyes slam shut, willing myself to sleep, but my eyelids flutter open again. Damn it! With a sigh, I throw the covers back and swing my legs over the edge of the bed. My head is pounding along with my heart. A conflicting mix of anger and...something else. It's a confusing warmth that spreads through me at the memory of Anna, a harsh contrast to the icy knot of betrayal that still lingers.

Anna's infiltrated my life again, her laughter echoing in every room, a constant reminder of the past. Earlier, I walked in to find her in a frilly cami and short set, a sight that shouldn't have ignited a flame of desire, but it did. I felt a primal urge to pull her close against me.

She barely looked older than Connor, with her face devoid of makeup and her chestnut hair falling in a messy tangle around her face. An image that shouldn't have stirred anything but a flicker of appreciation that she was comforting our child, yet my traitorous body had other ideas. I wanted to scoop her up in my arms and carry her to my bed.

God, I hate that I still desire her. How can I want a woman I can't trust?

But it's more than her appearance breaching my carefully erected defenses. It's the gentle way she soothed away Connor's fear. When I walked back in and overheard her reassuring our son that she and I both loved him, I felt the hard knot of betrayal in my chest loosen. She disarmed my own mother faster than I would have thought possible. Hell, she had Mom eating out of her hand by naming Connor after my father. That thoughtful gesture was a reminder of the woman I thought I knew. The woman who used to understand me. Damn her! How can she be all these wonderful things yet still be a woman who would cheat on her husband?

Grimacing, I rub the heel of my palm against my gritty eyes. The image of her lush body refuses to fade. I stretch my neck, trying to loosen the tension that's bunched my muscles into a knot. The bathroom offers a temporary escape. As I swallow the ibuprofen with a grimace, the chalky bitterness mimics the feeling in my gut. A bitter pill to swallow. That's how I feel. Who is the real Anna? The sweet girl I met on the cruise? The cheating wife or the loving mother who was comforting my son down the hall?

Shame burns in my throat, a bitter aftertaste of the confusing emotions swirling within me. How can I want someone I can't respect? Yet, I do. Sinking back onto the bed, I lean my elbows on my knees, the weight of the situation pressing down on me.

My son is the most important thing. I offered to let Anna stay because I thought it was best for him. Nothing changed. He loves his mother, and I can tell he needs her around. So, I can't ask her to leave just because I'm having difficulty resisting her charms.

No, instead, I need to guard my heart. Her warmth threatens to melt my icy defenses. She already hurt me once. She could do it again, leaving me with scars deeper than the ones I already carry.

My fist tightens around the bedsheet as I clench my jaw. This vulnerability, this confusing longing, is a weakness I can't afford.

My lips twist into a snarl. Where's the steely resolve I used to possess? Where's the man who navigated corporate battles with a cool head and an iron fist? Here I am, a CEO brought to his knees by... what? A memory? A ghost of the past?

"I must be getting soft," I mutter to myself, "What happened to my reputation for being stern and unyielding," my voice dripping with sarcasm. I can't let this mere slip of a woman get under my skin.

With that thought, I slide back on the bed and throw my arm over my eyes. The darkness offers only a temporary escape from the emotions raging within me.

My son's laughter wakes me the next morning. I blink as my eyes are gritty from lack of sleep. I resolutely stand and walk directly into the shower. I'm hoping the hot water will shake the fog from my brain.

Fifteen minutes later, I walk out of my bedroom, fully dressed and ready to face the day. The smell of sausage fills the air as I follow my nose to the kitchen. I walk directly to the coffee pot and fill my cup. I take a grateful sip before I turn to face my son's boundless energy and Anna's brief smile.

I hold up my hand and say, "We're meeting at your Uncle Chase's house tonight around six. I thought maybe you and I could shoot some hoops after breakfast."

"Cool," Connor offers his typical preteen response, but I can tell he's eager to go outside.

Anna deftly places a platter of scrambled eggs with cheese on the table. She returns with another plate filled with hash-browns and the perfectly browned sausage I could smell the minute I walked out of my room on the table. My stomach growls in anticipation.

I quickly dish up a portion for me, and Anna does the same. We've both learned to take what we want before my ever-starving son beats us to it.

"Thank you, Anna, this tastes good," I say politely. Connor glances over at his mom and says, "Yeah, Mom. Thanks."

"You're welcome," she hides a grin and gives me a wink. "Both of you."

Once we're done eating, Anna shoos us out the door with, "I'll take care of the dishes. You guys go play ball. I need some time this afternoon to get online and submit Connor's transfer to his new school."

"Let me know if you need assistance," I remind her, but she's already shaking her head. "No, but thanks. I've already been through this once."

Later, as Connor and I take the elevator to the apartment, we're both slick with sweat, our shirts clinging uncomfortably to our backs. A Florida afternoon spent playing basketball had left us thoroughly drained.

I smile over at my son. "Man, do we need a shower."

He lifts his arm for a sniff, then holds his nose in disgust. I laugh as I explain, "Yeah, we're a little ripe." His face falls into a frown, so I add solemnly, "That means we stink."

"Oh," he says with an agreeing nod.

We walk in to find Anna bent over in the pantry, head down, rummaging through the shelves. She straightens up quickly and turns around. Her cheeks are flushed from the exertion, "Oh, you're back. I hope you don't mind. I was just taking a look at your pantry, and it seemed a little cluttered. So, I took the liberty of reorganizing things a bit." She glances around defensively, then back at me, a sheepish grin on her face.

"Have at it. The kitchen is yours," I say with a sweep of my hand. She blinks in surprise. "Thanks, I appreciate that," I hear the sincerity in her voice.

As she walks over to hug Connor, she suddenly stops with a wrinkle of her nose. Connor looks up at her and states, "We're ripe." Then he gives her a wave and yells over his shoulder on the way into the bathroom, "I'm gonna take a shower."

"Good," Anna calls after him in a teasing tone.

I involuntarily smile. Then, as soon as I realize it, I frown. She looks at me as if I've lost my mind. "You okay?" she asks warily.

"Yeah, our son just wore me out. He's so full of energy, and I'm suddenly feeling my age." I say with a sigh. Anna smiles, "Been there, done that." She looks up at me with an apologetic smirk, "Hate to tell you, but it only gets worse."

Then she cocks her head and says knowingly, "It's worth it, though, isn't it?" She looks at me with a thoughtful gaze, "I shouldn't be surprised that you're both bonding so quickly. But I am."

"Bonding. Yeah, if that's what spending time with Connor does, then yes. It's totally worth it."

She gives me a sweet smile and looks like she wants to say more. I notice she has a smudge of flour adorably across her cheek, and I feel the urge to brush it from her. Instead, I abruptly turn on my heel, kicking myself for almost falling under her spell again. Then I stride to my bedroom and into a shower. A cold shower.

It's five thirty and Connor and I are waiting in the living room for Anna. We both hear a door open, and she steps into the living room, a vision in white. The light sundress whispers against her skin as she walks over to us. Its intricate purple flowers around the hem swirl around her legs. The delicate scent of lavender, perhaps from her shampoo, wafts past me.

"Mom, you look pretty," Connor says, a wide smile breaking across his face.

A light blush blooms on Anna's cheeks. "Thank you, honey. I made a little effort," she says, her gaze flickering nervously as she licks her lips.

She's pulled back her chestnut hair on both sides with combs, the style highlighting the light smattering of purple eyeshadow that deepens her clear gray eyes. With shiny lip gloss highlighting her full lips... *Kissable lips? What the hell? Seriously, Carson?*

I sigh, the sound escaping my lips before I can stop it. As I follow them out the door, I force myself to relax my shoulders, the tension momentarily forgotten under the weight of my traitorous thoughts.

I'm moodily silent on the way to my brother's house. "Dad!" Connor says loudly, as if it isn't the first time he's tried to get my attention. My eyes dart to the rearview mirror, catching a glimpse of his expectant face.

"Sorry, Buddy," I mutter. "I was miles away. I missed what you said."

"Uncle Chase is your younger brother, right?"

"Right," I confirm, forcing my attention back to the road. "There's two years between each of us. Chase is my youngest brother by four years, and Carter is in the middle. He's two years younger than me."

As Connor rattles off their names to himself, I reassure him, "Hey, don't worry about it. They'll all introduce themselves when we get there."

Anna and Connor both nod as I pull up to a large home in the San Marco area. It's an older historic district, and both my brothers have purchased homes in this area. I get out and open the door for Anna, a gentlemanly gesture despite my preoccupation. Connor is already bouncing on his feet. His hair is combed, and he's wearing cargo shorts like me. He is wearing a red T-shirt, and I'm wearing a light blue golf shirt. My heart swells with pride as he steps up beside me.

Before I can ring the doorbell, the front door swings open wide, and Chase and Carter stand crowded in the doorway. Val and Kat are behind them, peeking over their broad shoulders to get their first glimpse of their nephew.

Twelve

Anna

Connor's face breaks into a wide grin, his eyes sparkling with delight as he steps into the entranceway. He's immediately swept into the large family room, all the adults gathering around him in a circle.

My eyes quickly scan over Carson's two brothers. All the Knight men have similar coloring. Dark, almost black hair and bright blue eyes. They are all similarly tall, dark, and handsome.

"Damn, if you're not a chip off the old block," says Chase with a glance at Carson.

Carter steps forward. "I'm your Uncle Carter," he announces, "and this is your Uncle Chase," right before wrapping Connor in a hug. As he lets go. Chase steps forward, his voice husky with emotion. "Welcome to the family, kid."

Then, each of the women steps forward and follows suit. Kat, with her dark hair and cat-like green eyes, engulfs him in a fierce hug. Val comes up with the baby. "I'm your Auntie Val," she says, her dark wavy hair framing her dark eyes with deep dimples on both cheeks. She pulls him in with one arm for a side hug. "And this is your cousin, Gabriella. Gabby, meet Connor."

Gabriella reaches out with her baby hands and pats Connor's face. We watch as his eyes soften as he looks at her. He leans toward her, "Hi Gabby, I'm your cousin." He leans down and brushes her cheek with his hand. Little Gabby looks up at him with total fascination. Then she holds out her hands toward Connor, wanting to go to him, surprising both her parents.

"Oh, my gosh," Val exclaims. "Gabby never wants anyone else to hold her."

Connor's chest puffs out a little as he gives Gabby a lopsided smile. She gurgles and returns a toothless grin.

After all the introductions are over, Chase waves all of us into his huge backyard. A large covered deck with a fire pit and grill beckons us forward.

The entire backyard is a colorful oasis filled with all different types of flowers. A hint of honeysuckle sweetens the breeze, and the slosh of a water feature tucked into a corner of their high privacy fence adds the perfect background noise along with a touch of serenity.

We all take a seat around their large outdoor table as Val situates Gabby comfortably in her highchair. Chase disappears into the kitchen, emerging a few minutes later with a huge platter of steaks and a tray of vegetables. The sizzle of meat hitting the hot grill fills the air, mingling with the smoky aroma of charring steaks.

Carter and Carson, his hand resting on Connor's shoulder, join Chase around the now smoking grill. The guys each hold a cold beer in their hand while Connor is handed a wet can of soda from an iced cooler. They're engrossed in a discussion about the perfect char on a steak.

Val and Kat steal glances my way, their curiosity plain to see. Val is the first to break the ice. "Connor seems like a fine young man," she says. "I'm sure you're very proud."

I offer them both a tentative smile. "I am. Thank you."

Kat leans in with a friendly smile. "He resembles Carson. Bonnie had a family photo of the guys when they were younger. I swear he looks just like Carson did at that age."

"We spent the day with Bonnie yesterday," I share with them. "She showed us the photo and said the same thing."

"Oh, don't you just love Bonnie? She's the best mother-in-law," Val states with a fond smile.

Kat agrees. "She's been nice to me as well."

We make light small talk as the men continue to man the grill.

Val throws a glance over her shoulder at the smoky scene by the grill, then leans forward conspiratorially. "Speaking of family," she says with a grin, "the guys are talking about another cookout at Bonnie's place. It's quite a sight, all three brothers working the smoker together, dishing out mountains of food. They invite everyone – family, friends, neighbors. It's a real event," Val continues, her voice tinged with excitement, "and let me tell you, everyone has a blast!"

Kat joins in, a playful glint in her cat-like green eyes. "Everyone brings a covered dish, potluck style. And now that Carter has a motorboat, many people arrive at the party by boat. It's quite festive!" She glances over at my son, a warm smile gracing her lips. "I bet Carson can't wait to introduce Connor to the extended family. There are so many Knights in this town," she says with a slight shake of her head.

I sigh, a mixture of relief and nervousness washing over me. "Connor isn't used to having any family except me." I confide, "Carson and Bonnie have been showing him photos and he's loving it. Connor's eyes light up at every picture. He's asked a million questions about his aunts, uncles, and cousins." I shake my head gently, "It just about broke my heart to see him with his grandma. "

"Aw... I can only imagine," Val says with a loving smile as she reaches over and hands her little one a fuzzy toy. "I cried when she held Gabby for the first time."

A burst of laughter from the men shatters the comfortable conversation. "Ladies, the steaks are ready!" Chase announces with a grand sweep of his hand. "We have medium, medium-well, and well-done—"

"There's only one well-done, and that was made especially for you, Kat," Carter says with a teasing smile as he spears the charred piece and places it on a plate for his fiancée. "Thank you," responds Kat with a regal nod, a playful glint in her eyes. "As you wish," replies Carter with a wink that has Kat blushing.

We all chuckle at the obvious Princess Bride reference, a shared joke between the two. Kat grins at the good-natured teasing. I look around at the ease with which everyone talks to one another. Even Connor seems effortlessly woven into the fabric of this family. He belongs, while I... I do not. Their shared laughter is something I'm only a witness to.

A cold knot of isolation twists in my gut. I steal a glance around the table, the laughter and easy camaraderie a sharp contrast to the hollowness inside me. Like a child forgotten on Christmas morning, I feel a prickle of tears threatening to spill over. I'm the outsider.

My gaze darts to Carson. His eyes are fixed on me, an unreadable expression etched on his face. I quickly look away. My nerves are raw and vulnerable.

As the others continue to banter back and forth, I find myself daydreaming about what it would be like if Carson and I were a couple—a real family. I notice the way the Knight men adore their significant others. A stab of feeling, dangerously close to being jealousy, flashes through me. There was a time when Carson looked at me like that. He made me feel so cherished.

My mind drifts back to one drowsy afternoon when we were walking through a quaint town. I don't remember which town; its name lost in the passage of time. It had been a long, tiring day, but spending it with Carson made it enjoyable.

We found ourselves beneath the shade of a sprawling tree. Its wide branches shielding us from the bright sun. A soft breeze rustled the leaves overhead, carrying with it the salty tang of the nearby ocean.

Over cans of cold root beer, Carson shared his plans for the family business. His intense blue eyes blazing with a passion that made me smile. Even then, just by the way he spoke about his work, I knew he was destined for success.

His passionate speech eventually faded into a comfortable silence. Yawning, I must have drifted off to sleep snuggled against his broad shoulder.

Opening my eyes, I looked up to find his bright blue gaze fixed on me, an intensity that started a longing deep inside my heart. In the dappled sunlight filtering through the leaves and the sound of the ocean waves on the shore, I knew right then that I had fallen in love with him. In that stolen moment in time, I allowed myself to dream of forever—a future with Carson, bound together by love and commitment.

I hear a bark of laughter that immediately pulls me back to reality. I steal another wistful glance at Carson's family as they continue eating, laughing, and acting like the close-knit family I've always yearned for.

I shake my head ruefully. I learned a long time ago that daydreams are just that, unfulfilled dreams.

Plates clatter as I help clear the table. We all gather around the crackling fire pit, the flames casting a warm glow on everyone's faces.

Chase glances over at Carson. "You guys going to Wild Riders tomorrow night? I told Sam we'd all be there," he says, his gaze lingering pointedly on Connor.

Connor frowns, a furrow creasing his brow. "What's Wild Riders?" He looks up at his dad, a question mark etched on his face.

"It's a biker's bar that Sam, my uncle, and your great-uncle owns," Carson explains with a smirk on his lips.

"A biker's bar? Like motorcycles or bicycles?" Connor's innocent question elicits a round of chuckles from the men.

"Motorcycles, Connor," Carson clarifies, his smirk widening. "Definitely motorcycles."

"Really? Do you have a motorcycle?" Connor asks, his eyes wide with saucer-like wonder.

Carson nods. "Yeah, I have a bike, and so do both of your uncles." He lifts his chin in a gesture towards Chase and Carter. "And... so does Val. She rides a Spyder, the kind with two wheels in the front."

Connor's jaw drops in awe. "Cool!" he exclaims, glancing over at Val in disbelief.

Chase shakes his head with a chuckle, leans forward, and looks directly at Connor. "Would you like to see our bikes?"

Connor's eyes widen even further. He nods his head vigorously, bouncing with excitement.

Val glances at me, a knowing look in her eyes. "Go ahead, you should check out my Spyder," she says. "I need to put Gabby down for the night." We glance down at Gabby, now nestled in her mother's arms, her eyelids drooping sleepily. I offer a soft laugh. "Okay, I'll be right back."

Kat and I stand up and follow the men into the garage. Inside, two sleek motorcycles gleam in the dim light. One is a black Harley Davidson with "Chaser" emblazoned on the side in a stylish script. Val's machine stands beside it – a beautiful blue Spyder with "Bella" written across the side.

"These are amazing," I breathe, captivated by the chrome and leather machines.

As the men continue showing off their bikes to a wide-eyed Connor, Kat leans in and gives me a conspiratorial wink. "We can head back in," she whispers.

I offer her a grateful nod. "Don't worry," she continues, her voice barely above a murmur. "I doubt they even noticed we left. But honestly, even though I get a little bored with the motorcycle talk sometimes, it really is fun. I love riding behind Carter. I don't want my own bike, though. But if I did, it would definitely be a Spyder like Val's."

I nod in agreement. "I've never ridden on a motorcycle before," I confess.

"Shh..." Kat hushes me playfully. "Anna, don't let them hear you say that. They'll have you on the back of a bike in a heartbeat!"

I return her smile, a nervous flutter in my stomach. Turning to head back outside, Kat catches my gaze and gives me an earnest look. "Seriously, though," she says. "The Knight family is all about motorcycles."

Back outside, we find Val resting comfortably on a chair, her feet propped up. "Gabby, my precious little one, is fast asleep," she says with a loving smile. Then, seeing none of the men around, she leans in and lowers her voice. "So, Anna, what's going on with you and Carson?"

A blush creeps up my neck as their expectant eyes land on me.

Thirteen

Carson

As I pull out of the driveway and head home. I glance back at Connor. My son's eyes are heavy, but he's fighting sleep. We stayed late. Sitting around the fire pit eating s'mores and talking.

I glance over at Anna, who seems strangely quiet. I could tell something was bothering her tonight. "You okay?" I ask her. She avoids my eyes, "I'm fine. Your family seems nice. Very close-knit," she murmurs.

"Yeah, we are," I glance over at her again, but she turns to look out the window. My hands grip the steering wheel tighter, but I don't push. It's a silent ride home.

Once I unlock the door, Anna puts her arm around Connor, who is stumbling and half asleep. He finally mumbles, "Night," and walks into his bedroom. Later, we hear him in the bathroom. I go into his bedroom to say goodnight, and he's already dead to the world. I lean down and pull the covers over him.

After I close his door, I turn around to feel Anna slam into me. She stumbles and teeters backward. I quickly reach out, grab her arms, and pull her toward me to break her fall.

I almost groan when her soft curves collide with my hard body, which is getting harder. She's so close I can smell the scent of lavender in her hair. I feel her soft breasts pressed against my chest. My body's involuntary response is an unwelcome reaction to her nearness.

For one moment, I keep her held tight against me as I breathe her in. Then I force my arms to loosen so she can step back. My eyes rake over her white cotton cami and those ridiculously feminine shorts. I can see the dark shadow of her nipples through the thinness of the fabric. I swear they harden into peaks as my eyes catch on them. I pull in a ragged breath as I firmly put distance between us.

I feel my face harden as I struggle to control my intense desire. It burns through my gut, swift and sharp. I abruptly drop my hands as I step back. I don't even ask if she's alright. Instead, I turn quickly around and make a beeline for my bedroom.

As the door closes behind me, I grimace. Then I walk directly to the shower and turn it on. I put the water on cold and then reach in and turn it warmer. I quickly shed my clothes, step in, and soap up.

I grit my teeth as I reach down to take care of my uncomfortable hard-on. As the steam clouds around me, I stroke myself with one hand, the other pressed hard against the shower wall.

As I groan low in my throat, I get an image of Anna, her head thrown back, her eyes cloudy as she comes on my hard cock. Only as I crawl between the sheets do I realize her image was how she looks now, not her face as it was eleven years ago. *I am so fucked.*

I wake up to the sound of heavy and persistent rain lashing against the window. I stretch before peering out at the morning, shrouded in gray. I look up and see heavy storm clouds rolling overhead. Outside, the world is slick and glistening; it must have rained for most of the night.

Turning, I try to shake off my melancholy mood, which mirrors the dismal downpour of the relentless raindrops that stream past my window.

My steps feel heavy as I walk toward the kitchen. The rich aroma of coffee beckons me on. Anna stands rigid at the stove, her back to me. The only sound is the sizzle of bacon hitting the hot pan.

She pauses for a fleeting moment when she hears me at the coffee pot. However, she doesn't turn around as I pour myself a cup. The aroma of coffee, usually a comfort, does little to dispel the knot of unease in my stomach.

Connor rounds the corner, a frown marring his youthful face. "Why the sour face, Connor?" I manage a smile, getting down plates and handing them to him.

"It's raining," he mutters as if that explains everything. I hide a grin, remembering how I used to hate being cooped up when it rained, but that was before the wonderful invention of video games.

"Actually," I casually say, "I think I have a PlayStation around here somewhere."

Connor's eyes gleam. "You do? Where?"

"In my closet. I'll dig it out after breakfast. Deal?"

"Deal!" The frown vanishes in a flash, replaced by a bright smile as he bounces around, setting out the silverware. I shake my head, wishing I could change my mood as easily as he does.

Anna hasn't spoken a word to me this morning. Not a greeting, not a single glance in my direction. Part of me understands. Last night's chance meeting in the hall was a bombshell to my equilibrium and self-control. I can't blame her for steering clear of me.

Does she sense my frustration at what happened or what could have happened last night? I study her as she continues to deftly flip pancakes and fry up the bacon. I go over to the microwave and get out the warm syrup. No matter how she may feel toward me, she certainly doesn't let it affect the way she cares for me.

A guy could get used to hot breakfasts and home-cooked meals. We're all seated around the table and soon filling up on the golden-brown pancakes and crispy bacon. Anna again has three fried eggs on a plate for me, I notice with an appreciative grin.

Connor, bless his heart, seems oblivious to the tension. He grumbles about the rain but barely looks up from his plate. Almost as soon as we're done eating, Anna looks over at Connor, carefully avoiding my eyes. "I know you're dying to get to the video games, so go ahead. I'll take care of the cleanup."

Relief washes over me, a temporary reprieve from the awkward silence.

The rest of the morning melts away in a blur of button-mashing and friendly competition. Damn, the kid's good! He dodges and weaves through the virtual world with an agility that puts my aging reflexes to shame.

"Hey, Connor, we're tied!" I shout over the roar of the virtual battlefield, my hands still on the controller. "But you've won the last two rounds. You're a natural. Quick reflexes, sharp mind."

I turn and give him a high-five. A blush creeps up his cheeks, and his eyes practically sparkle. "Thanks, Dad," he mumbles with a hint of pride in his voice. "You're not too bad yourself... for an old guy."

I blink, a chuckle escaping my lips. Damn, if he isn't right. Compared to his ten years, I'm practically ancient. Still, his words warm me; they carry an acceptance that tugs at my heartstrings.

By lunchtime, thankfully, the relentless drumming on the roof finally seems to be tapering off. A weak stream of watery sunlight appears, peeking through the clouds and catching Connor's eye.

"Hey, it's stopped raining!" he exclaims, pointing excitedly towards the window. "Look, the sun's out."

It's a welcome change. Maybe a change of scenery is called for. That might be exactly what our unconventional family needs to break the tension. Simmering emotions seem to clog the air whenever Anna and I are in the same room, making it hard even to breathe.

"Great idea, Son," I reply, a smile tugging at the corner of my lips. "What do you say we give your mom a break from cooking and grab some lunch out?"

Connor practically rockets out of his chair. "Great!" he shouts, his enthusiasm echoing through the house. "Mom, Dad wants to go out for lunch!"

Anna's voice filters in from the kitchen, seeming muffled by the clatter of pots and pans. "Sure, that sounds good," she replies. But the forced cheer in her tone doesn't escape me.

The past few hours have been a whirlwind of domesticity—the shared breakfast and the video games with Connor. It's been... pleasant, a glimpse into a life I never dared to dream of. But Anna's silence, her studious avoidance of my gaze, hangs heavy in the air.

With a touch of frustration, I follow Connor into the kitchen. The room itself seems unchanged, the stringent aroma of cleaning solution replacing the earlier scent of bacon and coffee. But from where I stand, I can't quite see what Anna's been working on all morning.

Is she just cleaning and re-organizing the kitchen? Or is she doing it to avoid me? I grimace. Can I blame her? Isn't that what I was doing by playing video games all morning? At least it allowed me to bond with my son.

My eyes rake over her. I see the small frown lines between her clear gray eyes, and she looks... stressed. This can't be easy for her. They are having to move again. And she's being forced to share her son.

Shame washes over me, hot and unwelcome. I haven't really made things easy for her. With a sigh that rumbles deep within me, I make a silent vow. I have to try, for both our sakes, to navigate this minefield of emotions and make things smoother and less stressful - for both of us.

Her brow furrows in concentration, and she bites her lower lip. Stress shadows her eyes, but beneath it, I think I see a flicker of something else – a flicker of uncertainty?

She's as uncomfortable as I am. Maybe there is a chance for us to navigate this together.

"Anna," I start to move forward, my voice low and tentative. "Let me help you with that." It's a small gesture, a tentative offering of support, but it feels like a significant step forward.

Her eyes flicker to mine with a tinge of surprise. Then, a tentative smile graces her lips, taking the olive branch I'm offering. "Thanks," she murmurs, her voice softer than usual. "I wanted to move these pans to the lower shelf."

As I navigate around her in the cramped kitchen, our arms brush accidentally. It sends awareness slicing through me. An attraction that leaves me seeking more oxygen as I take in a deep breath. I grit my teeth, willing myself to focus on the task at hand. Grasping the heavy pans, I carefully transfer them to the lower shelf, keeping my movements controlled.

Once I'm finished, I step back. I glance around the kitchen, my gaze landing on the step stool she recently purchased from Amazon, now sitting in the pantry. A light bulb seems to turn on in my head. I reach for the cabinet knobs, opening a few to find them reorganized. She's relocated things, so they are all within her reach.

It dawns on me – she wasn't just avoiding me. She's settling in. She's carving out a space for herself within my home. I nod in silent understanding.

"You've been busy. This is really coming together," I say to her with an approving glance. She gives me a tentative smile. And suddenly, everything between us seems normal again. Then she turns around with a quick, "Let me just move this one skillet."

As she steps toward the still-open lower cabinet, I get a whiff of her lavender scent, which is uniquely hers. She bends over, her back to me, and instantly, my eyes go to her firm, rounded backside. My eyes linger on her sweet ass for a few minutes too long. And all my carefully controlled plans go instantly out the window. As my body wants to grab her by her hips—I suddenly hear a slight sound and remember Connor is with us, sitting at the kitchen counter.

He's doodling on a pad. Innocently unaware of the now different tension that wants to overtake my good intentions. Needing to resist it, I abruptly turn, walk out of the kitchen, and grab my keys.

"Everybody ready? Let's get out of here."

Fourteen

Anna

It's Friday afternoon, and a strange sense of harmony hangs in the air. I feel like there's been a subtle shift in my relationship with Carson. It started the other day. I don't know what happened, but Carson seems to have softened toward me.

It feels like a fragile peace, but I'll take it. I've heard back from the school, and somehow, I have a suspicion that Carson was involved. Connor will be starting fifth-grade classes next Monday at Bolles, a private school that offers excellent sports programs.

We've just returned from shopping, mostly for school clothes, because our moving boxes won't be delivered until early next week. But everything seems to be coming along. Each of us grabs a shopping bag as we head toward the elevator.

Connor suddenly spies a motorcycle parked off to the side. With his usual enthusiasm, he rushes toward it, eyes wide with admiration. "Hey, look. It's a Harley like Uncle Chase has."

Carson and I both stop as well. Connor continues to admire the sleek black Harley Davidson cruiser. I'm juggling the shopping bags when I hear Carson admit, "Yeah, it's mine."

"What? Really?" Connor, his eyes wide, turns toward Carson. "That's yours?"

Carson nods, "Yeah, I came down this morning and took the cover off it to make sure it was ready for tonight," he tosses the words out casually. "I thought you'd like to ride with me to Wild Riders."

My son's face lights up with excitement. "Really? Dad, that's so cool!" He turns to me, oblivious to the storm brewing inside me. "Mom! Did you hear that? I'm going on a motorcycle ride!"

I feel my face go pale as I imagine my son on the back of that... that machine. What if...? A wave of nausea washes over me, followed quickly by a wave of anger.

Connor doesn't seem to notice my lack of response. But Carson does. He glances over at me as I give a furious frown at his high-handedness. How dare he offer Connor a ride without consulting me first?

Without saying a word, I stalk toward the elevator, viciously jabbing the button. Distance is what I need right now. Otherwise, I will say something in front of my son, and he doesn't need to hear us arguing. And there *will* be an argument!

The apartment door slams shut behind me with a satisfying bang. I head straight for the laundry room. Ripping the new clothes off their hangers, I try to take deep, calming breaths, but the air seems thick with my pent-up rage.

My hands are shaking with my emotions as I brace my arms against the cold metal of the washing machine. I remind myself to be rational and to give Carson the benefit of the doubt. He's new to this whole parenting thing. Yet, my anger rises like a tidal wave, drowning out the voice of reason.

Suddenly, Carson enters, carrying the remaining shopping bags. He casts me a wary glance.

"I... uh... I told Connor he could shoot some hoops while we... talk."

I let my head fall forward between my arms as I take in a deep, shuddering breath. I will myself to not lose control as I straighten.

Lifting my head, I lock eyes with Carson. He seems to instinctively take a step back, his gaze flickering to the fury burning in mine.

"Did it not even occur to you to ask me first?" I prop my hands on my hips and advance toward him. "Before you volunteered our son for a joyride on that... that..." I struggle to find a word that adequately expresses my feelings. "That death trap?"

Carson has the grace to give me a sheepish look. "I'm sorry. Honestly, our entire family rides, so I didn't even think—"

"That's right. You didn't think!" I cut him off with righteous indignation. "He's ten years old, Carson! Ten! What happens if there's an accident? Motorcycles offer zero protection!"

"I bought him a helmet—" He cuts off his sentence the minute he realizes his words just added fuel to the flames.

"When? When did you buy my son a helmet?" I realize my mistake the minute the words leave my mouth. Carson, who was on the defense, suddenly stiffens. "Your son?" he questions in a sharp voice, his eyes like chips of ice. "He's my son too, Anna. In case you've forgotten."

My shoulders suddenly slump, "I know." I say quietly, my voice losing its earlier venom. "It's just... you can't just promise him things without consulting me first. And this is dangerous."

He nods and runs a hand through his hair, his shoulders tense. "I bought the helmet today. I wanted it to be a surprise. Asked the guy at the store what size to get while Connor was looking at shoes." He glances at me, his face devoid of emotion, "I had planned to show it to you first, but when Connor saw my bike..." He gives an apologetic shrug.

"I get it. I do," I say, raising my hands in a gesture of surrender, "It's just... I don't want to be the bad guy. The over-protective parent, who now has to tell him no." I feel my anger dissipate, replaced by a wave of exhaustion.

A flicker of understanding softens Carson's features. He steps closer, his voice gentler now. "You don't have to be the bad guy, Anna. We can figure this out together. Maybe we can find a compromise."

His words offer a lifeline, a way out of this emotional storm. Perhaps there is a way to negotiate this new reality, a way to balance safety with the desire to give Connor a taste of adventure.

"Maybe," I reply, a sliver of hope returning to my voice.

A hesitant smile touches Carson's lips. "Sounds like a plan. Now, how about we put these clothes away? Being a parent is hard work."

A reluctant smile tugs at the corners of my mouth. Maybe, just maybe, we can find a way to make this crazy, unexpected family we're building together - work.

It's just beginning to darken outside as I steal a glance in my bathroom mirror. A satisfied smile spreads over my face. I like the way my new outfit hugs my curves perfectly. Sometimes, I feel like everything I own screams 'Mom.' But my new black jeans and halter top don't even whisper the word.

I shake out my hair, letting it cascade down my shoulders. My silver earrings shimmer as they catch the light. Three coats of mascara later, my eyes are accentuated by a touch of smoky eyeshadow. A hint of blush and a touch of shiny lip gloss complete my transformation. I feel confident and attractive. Feelings I haven't embraced in a while.

When I expressed concern about Connor at a biker bar, Carson assured me that it's upscale, and besides, he and his brothers used to hang out there when they were teenagers. I thought about pointing out that Connor isn't a teenager but held my tongue. The man is already compromising on the motorcycle ride; the least I can do is put on a good face.

Walking into the living room, the conversation comes to a halt. Connor's eyes widen in surprise. "Gosh, Mom, you look amazing!"

A warmth spreads through me at his compliment. "Thank you, honey," I reply, trying to ignore the heat of Carson's gaze.

Connor's outfit is jeans and a T-shirt. Carson, standing beside him, practically oozes charisma tonight. His low-slung jeans hug his hips in a way that makes my breath hitch. His black T-shirt paired with the leather jacket screams bad boy charm. I discretely watch his masculine strides as we leave the apartment.

Connor, seemingly oblivious to the unspoken tension, casts a wistful glance at the Harley before clambering into the backseat of the SUV.

Pulling into Chase and Val's driveway, the garage door stands open, revealing Chase leaning against his motorcycle. Val emerges a few minutes later, a playful glint in her eyes as she hands Carson the keys to her Spyder.

"Take good care of my Bella, Carson," she says with a teasing lilt in her voice.

"Absolutely," Carson promises. He then turns his attention to Connor and assists him in securing the new helmet. Across the driveway, Chase throws a leg over his Harley, a picture of biker cool.

Thankfully, a quick Google search earlier today reassured me about the Spyder's safety features compared to a traditional motorcycle. Small victories, I remind myself.

Val and I head to her SUV, and she states, "Bonnie's watching Gabriella tonight. So, I'm treating this like a date night." She says as she throws a kiss at Chase.

"Thanks, Val, for letting Carson take your Spyder. I know I'll have to get used to the Knight family's obsession with motorcycles."

Val waves her hand dismissively. "Think nothing of it. I wouldn't ride at all while I was pregnant. Safety first." Her gaze flickers to me with a knowing glint. "So, I know you said there wasn't anything serious between you and Carson. Pity, by the way. But you should know that the air practically sizzles whenever you two are around each other."

I feel the heat rise in my cheeks, "We're attracted to each other, but I don't think Carson is willing to let go of the past." I see the question in her eyes, and I hold up a hand. "That's all you're getting out of me for now."

"Alright, I won't push it," she promises me with a grimace.

"So, tell me about Wild Riders. Carson mentioned it's upscale. That's kind of hard to imagine."

"Well, it's run by Sam Knight, their uncle. You'll like him," she says with a sideways glance. "He's a retired cop who is still active behind the scenes with the Jacksonville Sheriff's office."

"How does that work out with him owning a biker bar?" I question her.

"Exactly! He insists on anonymity for everyone who goes there, mostly for himself, I'm sure. So, everyone uses their biker nicknames." She shrugs.

"Really? Do all bikers name their motorcycles?"

"Wild Riders do," she says with a sly grin. "Since you don't have a bike, we'll call you and Connor by your names. But it's considered rude not to use everyone's nickname."

"Interesting. So, what are the names?"

"Chase goes by Chaser. No imagination." She rolls her eyes, "But most of the names have deeper meanings. Like mine, my dad used to call me Bella. Carter's name is Freedom, which is important to him. And Kat doesn't ride... yet. But you never know," she adds with a laugh.

The crunch of gravel announces our arrival at the parking lot. "Here we are."

I turn to get my first glimpse of Wild Riders. It looks like a converted warehouse. Wild Riders is written in bold letters across a large chrome sign. The front of the bar is adorned with flaming skulls and other types of biker paraphernalia.

As Val slams the car door, a handful of rough-looking men standing by their motorcycles turn to offer nods and smiles.

"Hi, guys!" She turns toward me, "This is Anna. She's with us."

Their gazes soften in respect as they each give me a nod. I return a tentative smile.

The guys pull in beside Val's SUV, and Connor hops off the back of the Spyder with a look of pure excitement. "That was awesome!" he exclaims.

We wait for them to secure their helmets before Carson pulls open the heavy oak doors.

The interior is surprisingly upscale. The wooden floors gleam with polish. There are spotlights strategically placed, and large flat-screen TVs adorn the walls, displaying a mix of silent motorcycle races.

Just before finding a seat, Connor asks, "Dad, where's the bathroom?"

"I'll show you," Carson says, turning to me. "We'll be right back."

I nod as we slide into a corner booth. A tall, broad-shouldered man approaches. He has silver hair, and he's sporting a goatee. In a booming voice, he says, "And who might you be, pretty lady?"

Chase states, "This is Anna." As the man turns to me, I state, "I'm here with Carson. We're old friends."

"Old friends, eh?" He says with a considering look, "From college?"

I blink at the abrupt question. "No. Not college," I stammer, caught off guard by the sudden shift in the conversation. "We met on a cruise. At a party. A masquerade party, actually."

At my words, the entire table falls eerily silent, and all eyes turn toward me. I try to hide my sudden nerves as the older man gives me an intense look, his gaze sharp under his bushy white eyebrows. Just as the silence starts to feel suffocating, a wave of relief washes over me as I see Carson appear behind the man, his hand resting on Connor's shoulder.

A hint of amusement dances in the older man's eyes, but I can't tell if it's directed at me or the situation. His voice cuts through the tension-filled air as he states, "Ah, here's Masquerade now."

Fifteen

Carson

I notice the tense silence as everyone turns to look at me. I notice Anna's eyes are wide and filled with surprise and something else I can't identify as she looks up at me.

"It looks like the cat's already out of the bag. Connor, this is Shadow. Shadow, this is my son, Connor."

"What did you just say? You're son?" My Uncle's eyes go wide in stunned disbelief.

I give my uncle a confused look, then smile. "Sorry, I thought that's what you all were talking about. This here is Connor Carlton. My son." I say with quiet pride.

My uncle chuckles, recovering, and pulls Connor into a warm embrace. "Boy, come here," he said, his gruff voice surprisingly tender. "I'm your great-uncle. Folks call me Shadow around here." His eyes give a suspicious shine as he says solemnly, "Your grandpa was my brother. A good man, taken too soon. Now, let me take a look at you." He steps back. "You carry a mighty fine name there, young man. How old are you?"

Connor grinning from ear to ear. "I'm ten years old," he states proudly.

"Ten, you say?" Sam rumbles, a hint of raw emotion lacing his voice. "You're awfully tall for your age." He ruffles Connor's hair affectionately, a small smile playing on his lips.

Conner doesn't even try to duck his head. "Mind if I show the kid around?" He glances from me to Anna. We both smile and shake our heads no.

After Sam leaves, I slide into the booth beside Anna. Her thigh is pressed against mine. I watch as she tries to subtly shift closer to the wall.

We all look up as Spitfire, a burly man, approaches the table. A tray balanced on his wide hand, a bandana tied securely around one thick arm. He places a frosty beer in front of each of us. As he sets one down in front of Anna, he says, "I'm Spitfire, and since this is your first time here, it's on the house." He glances at Val with a twinkle in his eye, "Gave away your Shirley Temple to the boy."

Val's laughter fills the air as she explains to Anna, "That's what he served me while I was pregnant." She eagerly reaches for the mug, the clinking glass joining the sound of our laughter.

Anna, however, remains uncharacteristically subdued. She hesitantly picks up her beer, taking a small, tentative sip.

Just then, Carter and Kat arrive, their entrance momentarily diverting my attention. We all shuffle to make space, and Anna once again finds herself pressed close against me. I fight back a smile at her flustered expression.

"Sorry, we're late." Carter waves to Spitfire and holds up two fingers. He immediately comes over with another frosty mug for my brother and a white wine for Kat.

"Did we miss anything?" Kat asks after Spitfire disappears with a smile.

Chase clears his throat but doesn't say anything; instead, he gives me a contemplative look. Val, however, leans toward Kat and says in a stage whisper, "Shadow was just asking Anna how they met." She nods to me and Anna. My stomach tightens at her words. "Anna said they met on a cruise." I let out the breath I was unconsciously holding. Then Val leans forward again, "At a masquerade party."

Well, shit! I glance over at Anna, who has a blush of color on her cheeks. She's toying with her mug of beer. I look at the others who have turned their attention to me, curiosity written all over their faces. Every. Damn. One. Suddenly, I'm the one squirming uncomfortably in my seat.

I glower at each of them, daring them to ask me outright. I pick up my beer and down half the glass.

Carter, probably taking pity on me, interjects, "Connor said you promised to take him out on the boat."

"Yeah, I was hoping I could take him out this weekend. If you hadn't made plans."

He waves his hand, "Nah. Go ahead. Kat and I thought we'd take a drive down to Goldhead State Park this weekend. Maybe hike down the ravine."

As the conversation turns to state parks, I breathe a sigh of relief, but I still feel Anna's eyes as she occasionally glances over at me.

My uncle comes back with Connor in tow. "Gave him the nickel tour. He wouldn't mind playing a game of pool." He hints with a wink in my direction.

Instructing Connor on the rules of the game of pool offers a welcome distraction. He soaks up the lesson with wide eyes, his face a mixture of concentration and delight as he sends the colored balls scattering across the green felt. Each successful pocket garners a joyous shout, each miss a crinkled brow and a determined pout.

Chase has taken over coaching duties, leaving Carter and me leaning against the wall, silent observers. I can practically feel Carter's scrutiny burning a hole into my side. Finally, I met his gaze, my voice tight with anticipation. "Just spit it out," I said.

Carter gives a slow nod. "Alright, fine. Here goes. I can't help but wonder why you haven't asked Anna to marry you."

A frown etches itself onto my face, but I remain silent. He pressed on, his voice laced with a hint of confusion. "There's an obvious spark there, wouldn't you say? You haven't taken your eyes off her all night, and there's a certain familiarity between you both. Plus, you're already living together. So, I'm just curious."

His words hang heavy in the air. I cross my arms, mulling them over. The truth is, the idea of marriage has crossed my mind. But the past looms large, too significant to ignore. Vows mean nothing to Anna, and that holds a weight I simply don't want to accept.

Finally, I comment, my voice flat. "We're not having sex."

Carter shoots me a surprised look. "Ah. That explains the tension, then." He holds his hands up defensively as I glare at him. "Hey, it's thick enough to cut with a knife, Bro'. Honestly, I'm a little surprised. Given your history, I figured—" He cuts himself off, a flicker of apology in his eyes. "Sorry, didn't mean to overstep. Trust me, living with Kat and not sleeping together was pure torture. But it wasn't long after I moved in that things escalated."

I sigh, offering a weak excuse. "It's complicated. Anna and I have a child together; it would make things awkward."

"Sleeping with her would be awkward," he counters, a knowing glint in his eyes. "Wouldn't it be more accurate to say sleeping with her *again* would be awkward?"

Silence hangs heavy between us as I consider his words. Carter finally shrugs, his voice softening. "Look, all I want is for you to be happy. You and Connor, that's a beautiful thing to see.

But being with Kat has shown me what it's like to truly love someone. And let me tell you, it's pretty damn amazing. I just want you to have that same kind of happiness."

"Yeah, well... you love Kat." Carter nods again, "Yes. I do. But I was in love with her for a while before I finally admitted it to myself."

A thoughtful silence stretches between us, broken only by Connor's triumphant yell as he sinks a shot. Carter squeezes my shoulder in a silent display of camaraderie before we both turn towards Connor, ready to shower him with praise for his newfound pool skills.

Carter and Chase amble back to the booth, rejoining the girls who are having a lively conversation. Connor and I volunteered to take care of the pool cues. An older gentleman with a cane shuffles past, his steps slow and measured. Connor's gaze lingers on him even after he disappears around a corner.

"Hey, Son, you alright?" I ask, placing a hand on his shoulder. "Did you recognize that man?"

Connor shakes his head. "No, he just reminded me of Graham. I mean, I was just a little kid when he died, but Mom has pictures of him." A shrug follows, his youthful expression clouded with a fleeting shadow.

With a frown, I ask carefully. "How old was Graham?"

"I don't know," Connor mumbles, his voice barely above a whisper. "I overheard someone say he was too old to be married to my mom..."

"And that bothered you?" I prod, the cue sticks forgotten in my hand.

He hesitates, then shakes his head again. "Not really. It was what they called Mom that made her cry. They called her a gold-digger." He gives me a soulful look,

"Words can be hurtful, huh?" I murmur, focusing on him only. I pull him into a comforting side hug. I say in a low voice, "Here, why don't you hang these up?" I hand him the cue sticks, trying to steer the conversation away from his memories.

I blink to dispel the red haze, trying to cloud my eyesight. A small smile begins and spreads across Connor's face, the past forgotten. If only it were that easy for me, I think, with a scowl. Anna's past is a tangled web of secrets and betrayal. And it stands between us, casting a long shadow over the present.

Leaving Wild Riders, Connor again rides behind me on the Spyder. I can tell he loves the freedom of the bike, as the wind sails by us. My mind continues to churn over what he told me.

I don't like the picture it paints of Anna. In no time at all, we're pulling up at Chase and Val's house. We park the bikes. Chase heads over to us, his cell phone to his ear.

"Hey, Mom asked if Connor wanted to spend the night. We're headed over to pick up Gabby so we can drop him off."

Anna and I both look over at Connor. He gives a delighted grin. "Sure, I'd like to spend the night at Grandma's." He looks up at me, "We're going out on the boat tomorrow, right?"

"Yes, that'll work out perfectly." I give him a hug, and then Anna leans down with a soft kiss, "Behave. I'll bring your swim trunks with me tomorrow."

They pile into the car as we wave goodbye. The ride home is filled with an unspoken tension. I reach down and turn up the radio as I don't feel like talking.

It's only after I close the apartment door behind us that Anna stops and turns toward me—a challenge on her face, mixed with a glimmer of what could be hopefulness. It only hardens my heart.

"You named your bike Masquerade?" She asks me, even though it's not phrased as a question.

I feel my face tighten, "Yes," I frown down at her, "As a reminder... never to trust too easily." The words spoken cruelly—like weapons, meant to hurt her. I should feel satisfaction when they do. Her eyes darken as the barbs hit home.

She swallows hard, gives me a nod, and starts to turn away wearily.

Yet, I can't stop more harsh words from tumbling out, "Gold-digger, that's quite a label. Makes me wonder about Graham's age and money. Feeble old man, or just plain old?" Her pale face does little to quell the storm brewing within me. "How old was he, Anna?"

"Why would you ask that?" She demands softly.

I fire back, my voice cutting, "Because I want to know."

She finally answers in a low but steady voice, "He was seventy-two."

I feel my lips twist into a snarl. "No wonder you went looking for sexual satisfaction elsewhere."

Her head jerks backward as if I slapped her. I watch as the rage gathers; her clear gray eyes turn dark and stormy.

"You have no right to judge me," she states in a furious tone as she moves quickly toward me. "None."

As she lifts her chin with a defiant look, I suddenly can't take it. I reach out and pull her roughly into my arms. I silence her gasp with a hard and punishing kiss. I shouldn't be feeling this overwhelming attraction to someone I don't respect.

I feel her moment of surrender as she softens against me. I reach up, grab a fistful of her hair, and pull her head back so I can see her eyes. They are still cloudy, but not from anger. "Is this what you want? Does this turn you on, Anna? Do you like it rough? Do you get off on hate sex?"

Her eyes narrow, looking directly at me. "Is that what you need to call it, Carson?" She taunts me back. I tug harder on her chestnut hair, exposing her slim neck, and lean down, my teeth graze over her soft skin. I quickly pull her halter top over her head and push up her bra, exposing her lush breasts. I grasp her breasts with my hands. Squeezing them roughly.

When I hear her low moan of arousal, I quickly divest her of her black jeans, leaving her standing before me in her silky black underwear. My gaze rakes over her hotly. I watch as her nipples pebble. I reach out and circle her areola, and then I pinch her nipple just enough to elicit a gasp.

I feel my already hard cock throb, impatient to be inside her. "Is that why you allowed me to fuck you, Anna?" I taunt, my voice cruel. "Because he couldn't?"

Her eyes practically ignite with rage at my crude words. "No," she steps back, out of range of my touch. "I slept with you because I had fallen in love with you."

My outstretched hand falls to my side in shocked denial at her words. Their meaning is like a bucket of cold water thrown at me. I just look at her, my mouth practically hanging open. I watch as she bends down and regally picks up her discarded clothes. She turns without once glancing my way and walks toward her bedroom; her head held high.

I hear her door close with a soft thud and then a click as she locks her bedroom door.

Sixteen

Anna

Oh, God. I shouldn't have admitted that to him!

I lean back against the door, my legs still weak with desire. In my mind's eye, I still see the look of contempt on Carson's face. Even knowing how he feels about me, I wanted him to make love to me... only it wouldn't have been love. No, what did he call it? Hate sex.

I give a silent laugh. I look down at my clothes which are still in my hands. Then look down at my body to see my black bra still pushed up over my breasts. My nipples are hard from his touch. My entire body is left aching. There is a pulsing between my thighs from desires unfulfilled. I press my legs together, hoping to assuage the need.

Damn you, Carson. Damn you for making me want you.

I think back over his questions; the word gold-digger, surprisingly, still holds the power to sting.

There was only one person who called me that, and his opinion was expected. It was too soon after Graham's death, and I was still stricken with grief.

So, when his stepson flung those words at me and left, I cried. Tears streamed down my face as I held Connor, his whimpers a reflection of my own distress. I buried my face in his soft hair, finding comfort in rocking him back and forth. In that moment, the four-year-old in my arms offered more solace than any adult.

As an only child, I was a surprise to my parents, who were already in their forties when I arrived. Their friends, all mature and established, doted on me throughout my childhood.

My first memories of Graham were filled with joy. He and his wife, Martha, were my parents' best friends, and they would shower me with fifty-cent pieces during visits. Graham's laugh would sweep through the room as he'd scoop me up and spin me around. He was like a favorite uncle, a source of unconditional love and amusement.

I was twenty when my parents were both killed in a car accident. My father somehow lost control of the car, and they slammed into a tree. Graham, now a widower, as Martha had passed seven years before, stood by my side at their funeral. He was a pillar of strength and support. As the harsh reality of their lack of life insurance and a heavily mortgaged house sunk in, I struggled. He offered not just emotional support but financial guidance as well.

He was helping me find an affordable apartment when he got his first diagnosis of cancer.

While Graham was old, he had never seemed frail. Now, a noticeable decline in his vitality cast a shadow over his once vibrant spirit. I ended up moving in with him as his health failed.

When Martha and Graham married, she had an adult son, Neal. The stepson and Graham never got along. Neal had stolen money from the couple's savings account because he battled a gambling addiction. When Martha died, Graham attempted to distance himself from his stepson without success. When Neal discovered Graham was ill, not once did he offer support, not even when Graham's cancer took a turn for the worse.

I took a job as a barrister because the flexible schedule allowed me to become Graham's primary caregiver, taking him to treatments and countless doctor visits. One particularly grueling day after chemo, a weak Graham informed me that he had contacted his lawyer. He was leaving his entire estate to me.

Feeling stunned and humbled, I assured him that I'd take care of him no matter what. "Annie," he rasped, his voice weak but his eyes filled with affection, "you've always been like family to me."

The lawyer, a friendly man with a reassuring smile, arrived to solidify Graham's wishes. He listened attentively as Graham outlined his plan. However, the lawyer pointed out a significant hurdle. Due to Graham's ten-year marriage to Martha, her stepson could potentially contest the will, especially considering Graham's weakened state.

Graham stubbornly demanded a foolproof way to ensure I inherited everything. He was adamant that as his full-time caregiver, I should be able to quit my job. The lawyer handled the legality of everything. He established a salary for me while strongly recommending marriage to avoid any future challenges from Neal.

At first, Graham and I were both vehemently against the idea. Marriage felt wrong to both of us. However, with his stepson already inquiring into Graham's finances, we both caved.

That didn't stop Neal from prolonging the settlement of the estate for years after Graham's death. It was a long and stressful battle. At times, I almost threw in the towel and let him inherit. It was only Graham's dying wish that kept me steadfast.

I shake my head to clear away the old memories that shroud the present like a fog.

I glance at my bedside clock. It feels like hours have gone by as I reminisced over decisions made in the past. Instead, I'm stunned that it's only been mere minutes... I'm suddenly aware that my body is still humming - like a live wire, from my pent-up desire. I drag in a few deep breaths, but I'm still unable to calm down.

I decide on a glass of white wine. Maybe it will relax me enough to sleep.

Decision made: I hold my breath and listen for any sounds in the apartment. It's silent, except for the beat of my heart. Carson must be in his bed. I pull off my bra but leave on my panties and throw on a robe. I warily open the door and listen again. Silence greets me, so I step into the hall and pad barefoot to the kitchen.

I turn on a single light to help locate a glass. I open the fridge and grab the bottle of white wine. After I've filled my glass, I take a sip. The chilled liquid feels good as it glides down my parched throat. I savor the taste, waiting for it to calm my frayed nerves. Being careful not to make a sound, I tiptoe back through the living room.

I nearly spill my wine as a silent shadow rises from the armchair. I feel my heart start to thud as the soft light from the kitchen illuminates Carson's harsh and slightly cruel features.

"If you thought your admission would soften my feelings toward you... you were wrong," he grates out.

Too late, I realize the danger. I thought Carson was safely in his bedroom. Instead, it appears he's been sitting in the dark, brooding and drinking. I spy the half bottle of scotch and an empty glass near his chair. He slowly approaches with a grace that reminds me of the caged cats at the zoo. When they stalked their prey. Suddenly, my throat is dry again.

"Put down the wine, Anna," my eyes fly to his. I soundlessly place the glass on the coffee table without turning my back on him. A shiver of apprehension travels down my spine as he moves closer. "You should never try and lock me out. I own everything in this apartment. I hold all the keys." His voice is low and has a menacing quality to it. I shiver outright as his heated gaze rakes over me.

His hand reaches out and unties my robe, pulling it open until it slides off my shoulders and onto the floor with a whisper of silk. I stand before him, my only barrier a small scrap of black lace around my hips.

"If you had feelings for me back then, you should welcome my touch." He says silkily as his hands come out to fondle my breasts. My traitorous body immediately responds, and my nipples turn into hard peaks. He gives an arrogant laugh, and my cheeks burn from his high-handedness.

"I cared for you then, Carson. I... I don't care for you anymore." I try to say bravely, but the slight quiver in my words gives me away.

"No?" He taunts me. I swallow as Carson, in this mood, is dangerous. All my senses are on high alert.

"No. I... I hate you right now, Carson." I cross my arms over my breasts and raise my chin in a defensive gesture.

"Hate. That's a powerful word, Anna," he says smoothly, with a glint in his eyes. "Especially when we were talking earlier about hate sex."

I smell the alcohol on his breath, and he again stalks me as if I'm his prey. He steps around me, moving closer. He's so close that I feel his hot breath on my neck and the heat of his body against my bare back. I shiver in response. He reaches out and brushes my hair to the side. I feel his lips as they skim over my shoulder, the sensation leaving goosebumps on my skin. Again, he softly chuckles like a cat playing with a mouse. I feel helpless under his insolent gaze.

I shut my eyes, knowing I never should have told him how I felt back then. I should have known he would use my feelings against me. That's what he's doing right now. Damn him.

"Hate sex could be good. Maybe even great. What do you think, Anna?" He murmurs in a husky voice. "You see, I'm getting tired of having to control my body's response when I'm around you. We're good in the sack. Why shouldn't we enjoy the pleasure we can give each other?"

Again, I can't form a coherent word. I just shudder from his warm breath against my ultra-sensitive skin. He steps around until I'm facing him.

He slowly reaches down and picks up a lock of my long hair. He plays with it, then lets it fall, only to wrap a fist full around his hand and use it to pull my head back slowly. I feel the sting against my scalp, just like before, but this time, his movements are controlled and deliberate.

His eyes gleam with satisfaction as I open my mouth to draw in a shaky breath. "That's it, Anna," he says as he pulls me forward by his hand in my hair. He presses me into his body, and I feel his hard rigid cock. He rubs my hips against his. My panties dampen with need.

I wonder where my willpower has gone as I stand there feeling helpless in his arms. God help me. It's been so long. I want this. I want him; the throbbing between my legs intensifies as he dominates my traitorous body. I let out a whimper as his hand tightens in my hair.

"I can tell you want me." His hand finds my breasts again, and he takes his time, cupping each one and rubbing my already-sensitive nipples with his thumb. "You like it when I do this, don't you, Anna?" He leans forward and covers a nipple with his mouth. He lightly grazes it with his teeth. I gasp as an uncontrollable tremor racks my body. "You like it when I'm rough," he says with a satisfied twist of his lips.

His face looks emotionless except for the heat in his eyes as he watches the way my body involuntarily responds to him. He has every right to look superior, as I feel like I'm a puppet on a string.

He suddenly gets even bolder as his hand goes up my back and around my neck, pulling me toward his hungry mouth. Then his lips are on mine, and I can't think. I can only feel as he pushes his tongue inside and possessively sweeps my mouth.

When he finally raises his head, I pull in a ragged breath. I feel his hands grip my ass as he again grinds me hard against him. I let out a soft moan, and he offers a satisfied smirk.

His grin widens as I press my thighs together. "That won't help, Anna. You need to spread your legs for me." He suddenly swings me around so that I'm facing the arm of the couch. He presses against my lower back, bending me over and positioning me where he wants me.

My hands automatically go out as I brace myself against the cushioned arm. My hips are higher than my head, and my hair falls forward like a curtain around my face. He pulls my panties down around my thighs, but he doesn't take them off. As I start to lift back up to remove them, he stills me with pressure on my back.

"No, leave them where they are," he orders in a gruff voice. They are wrapped around my thighs but not too tight. He steps back, and I instantly miss his sensual touch on my skin. I feel like a drug addict longing for a fix.

I hear his smug, satisfied voice behind me. "You should see how you look to me, Anna. Your hair messy, your black panties down around your thighs, and your perfect ass." I feel his hand as it glides over an ass cheek. "You look so fuckable right now. You're ready for me, aren't you?" I can't answer. I'm slightly panting with anticipation from his dirty words.

I hear the sound of his zipper being lowered. My senses are on overload. I feel so vulnerable bent over like this, waiting for him to claim me. Aching for him to take me. I've gone from damp to drenching wet.

He continues in a voice that's grown tight with his arousal, "I want to watch my hard cock sliding in and out; I want to watch my cock as I fuck you." I let out a whimper as his words paint a vivid, sensual picture in my mind. Then, both of his hands wrap around my hips roughly. I feel his body warmth as he steps in close. Finally, my mind screams. Take me. Hurry. Please. Why is he hesitating? In the semi-darkness, I let out another desperate whimper of need as I wait.

Seventeen

Carson

I look down at Anna, and she's practically begging me to take her. Now, it's time for me to walk away and leave her aching for me.

When I saw her making her way to the kitchen, I cooked up this little plan for revenge. I would get her to this point of no return and then leave her wanting, panting, needing me.

The problem is—my plan has backfired. I don't think I'm capable of walking away. I want her too damn much. I could pound nails with my hard-on. Just the thought of my cock plunging into her has me shaking with need. Why shouldn't I take what she's willing to offer? I reason.

I move closer, my engorged cock pulsing and eager. I fist it with one hand as I position myself at her core, and hearing her needy whimper, I can't wait another minute. I thrust forward, she's so damn tight, I have to pause. I pull out a bit and then thrust heavily into her again.

When I'm finally in full throttle, I groan at the feeling. "So, fucking, good," I mutter in a gravelly voice. I pull out and then push roughly back in, setting a rhythm. I look down and watch my cock as it enters her, a visual stimulation that mixes with the sounds and the feeling of sliding into her wet warmth.

I tighten my grip on her hips to hold her steady as I increase the pace. Soon, I'm slamming into her, the sound of our bodies as they make contact only increasing my need. I'm practically pushing her off her feet with the forcefulness of my thrusts. Yet, she pushes back to meet me halfway.

I'm close. I feel my balls pull up and tighten. I hear her pants as the first tremor courses through her body. Then she lets out a shout as her body clamps down hard. Milking me. I follow her over the edge with a hoarse groan of completion. I lean over her bare back. Spent. It takes a few moments to recover from my mind-blowing orgasm.

I finally straighten, pulling her up beside me. I wait for us to recover as our breathing slows.

As I hold her against me, the realization slams into me. I should never have tried to use our desire as a weapon. It's a double-edged sword. As my mind clears, the knowledge hits me; I've never known this type of chemistry, this connection, whatever the hell you want to call it, with any other woman. I feel slightly ashamed. I was so keen on revenge that I was willing to use sex as a weapon against her.

I lean down and press my forehead against her hair in an unspoken apology. She's still turned away from me, but I have my arms around her, pressing her back against my chest.

"Anna, this chemistry between us. It's... unique. I promise I'll never try to use it against you. Okay?" I let out a sigh at her silence. "Resisting it is torture. So, instead, I think we should just accept it. Give in to it. Be lovers." I stop for just a moment, then continue, "Look. Don't answer right now. I just want you to think about it."

I feel her nod her head in agreement. I reluctantly let go of her, stuff myself back into my pants, and pull up my zipper.

She's in front of me, bare except for her panties, a thin strip of black still around her thighs. And damn if I don't want her again. But I took her so roughly she'll probably be sore in the morning. Hell, she's probably sore right now.

I have a strong urge to pick her up and carry her to my bed. Just to keep her close. Instead, I loosen my hold on her. She looks a little lost, and I see her face flush red when she sees I'm still fully dressed.

I suddenly don't want her to feel used. I lean down and softly brush my lips over hers. I pick up her robe, wrap it around her shoulders, and walk with her back to her bedroom. As I leave her at her door, I look down into the clear gray of her eyes.

"I want you to consider my suggestion, Anna. I'd like us to share the master bedroom." With that, I brush her cheek with my hand, turn, and walk away, giving her time.

As I shut my bedroom door behind me, I shake my head ruefully. *Way to teach her a lesson, Knight. Instead of pushing her away, you invite her into your bed.*

I suddenly grin as the thought doesn't seem too bad. In fact, it feels... right. I crawl between the sheets and don't stir until morning.

There's a dull throb behind my eyes due to the amount of scotch I drank the night before. No regrets, though. A smirk plays on my lips as I head for the shower.

After getting dressed for a day on the water, I head to the kitchen, unsure what to expect from Anna this morning.

The aroma of bacon hits me, drawing my smile even wider. My steps quicken as I find Anna in the kitchen, her figure accentuated by a light summer top. It shows off her curves in a way that makes me want to strip it off her.

She turns, a soft smile gracing her lips. "Good morning," she says, her eyes slowly skimming down my body before coming back to mine.

"Yes, it is," I reply, my grin mirroring hers. "Haven't felt this good in a while."

She pulls her eyes away as she turns to the skillet in front of her. "Scrambled eggs with cheese?"

"Sounds great," I fill my cup with coffee and then pour her a cup. I help her bring the food to the table.

We both fill our plates and start eating. The silence isn't strained. Instead, it feels... expectant. The air practically thrums with hopeful energy, a shared anticipation for what the day, and perhaps the future, might bring. Neither of us mention last night.

I steal a glance at Anna. Searching for a clue in her expression. When I don't find one, I glance away. "Is there anything we need to grab for Connor?" I ask casually, not wanting to push.

"No, I already have his swim trucks. I grabbed some towels, and I thought maybe I'd pack a few treats. I know Connor will want to snack. I didn't pack a lunch, though."

"That works," I shrug. "I'll help clear the table, and then we can head out."

On the way over to my mother's, we stop to grab a bag of ice and some canned drinks. I pop the trunk and throw everything into the large cooler I brought. We don't talk, but the silence isn't strained. I turn up the music.

My mom greets us at the door. "Connor is in the kitchen," she says with a smile. I made chocolate chip cookies."

"I hope you made enough for us to take some on the boat," I ask with a hopeful smile.

"Of course, I already have them in a container for you," she says with a fond smile. "Thanks for letting Connor stay over. It was nice to make breakfast for someone besides myself."

Anna answers for both of us, "Anytime, Bonnie. We can make it a regular thing if you want, or just play it by ear?"

"Maybe every other weekend while he's still young? I know once he's older, he'll be too busy with school, sports, and girls to want to spend too much time over here."

Anna and I chuckle. "I hope that won't be for quite some time," I say with a grimace.

Connor is sitting in the kitchen with a happy grin on his face and a smear of chocolate around his mouth. "You ready for a boat ride?" I ask him.

"Yes!" His eyes go to Anna, "Did you bring my swimming trucks?"

She hands him a bag, and he whoops and disappears into the bedroom to change. A few minutes later, he emerges in his blue swim trunks, sunglasses, and flip-flops. Anna says, "I brought all of us a towel, and I also brought you a T-shirt."

As we walk toward the boathouse, the sky overhead is a bright, cloudless blue, matching my cheerful mood.

After we transfer everything to the boat, we wave goodbye to my mom, and I push the throttle forward. The engine offers a deep rumble as it roars to life. As the boat picks up speed, the wind whips past us, carrying a hint of salt and pine—Anna's long hair streams behind her as she lifts her face to the sky. A light spray of water shines on our cheeks as it's kicked up from the bow.

"Dad. Can I steer the boat?" Connor yells over the rumble of the engine. His eyes raised in a hopeful expression.

I promise him with a grin, "Sure, once we get to more open water, you can take over." His eyes shine with anticipation.

Soon, we're in a wider part of the river, and I turn to Connor as I slow the boat. The noise of the engine softens to a quieter hum. "Okay, put your hands on the wheel," I instruct him. He steps in front of me, his excitement obvious. "This is the throttle. Push forward to make the boat go faster and pull it back to slow it down."

Connor listens intently, paying careful attention. I let him take over the wheel, standing behind him and offering patient guidance with my hand on his shoulder. He steers with surprising confidence, a wide grin splitting his face as the boat moves forward, carving a path through the blue water.

My eyes cut to Anna, who is smiling. She gives us a thumbs-up, her easy-going manner as refreshing as the wind. A carefree smile spreads across my face in response. Any tension that may have lingered between us seems to melt away, dispelled by the bright sun and the rhythmic pounding of the boat on the waves.

After a few hours, I instruct Connor to navigate the boat over to a wide part of the river. Then we drop anchor. I pop open the cooler while Anna pulls out some snacks. After we've munched on fruit and crackers, Anna insists that Connor needs more sunscreen.

I walk up behind her and murmur, "Would you like me to put lotion on your back?"

She takes off her light summer shirt, revealing a dark purple bikini top that hugs her curves. Her shorts are purple and white, and they show off her long, tanned legs. When I step up behind her, a sensual awareness seems to simmer between us.

She hesitates for just a moment, the breeze carrying the sound of birds chirping on the nearby shore. "Sure," she turns around, her voice a touch breathless.

I warm the lotion in my palm, and the sound of the waves lapping against the boat creates a rhythmic background hum. "I'll be very thorough," I warn, my voice husky.

She closes her eyes as I begin, and a shiver runs down her spine as I reach her lower back. A soft breath escapes her lips. I move slowly and sensually, the warmth of her skin sending a current through me. Her hair falls around her face, framing her in a way that makes me wish we were alone. I want to pull her close and kiss her, but I force myself to focus on the task at hand.

By the time I'm done, I feel more affected by the contact than she does. Or maybe not? A hint of a blush on her cheeks and a soft smile playing on her lips. She pulls her hair into a messy bun, a few tendrils escaping to frame her face. She looks irresistible, and I have to force myself to look away. There will be time for more later... I hope.

Connor, his eyes wide as saucers, swivels in his seat, scanning the horizon like a young pirate searching for treasure. He loves being out on the water – keeping up a constant chatter as he asks questions about the different wildlife and what creatures live beneath the river's surface.

There are 'No Wake' signs in certain places on the river, so I explain, "We need to be careful in these areas, Connor." Pointing to a sign. "See that warning? It means we need to slow down to protect the manatees. They're gentle giants, but our boat's propellers can hurt them."

His eyes grow solemn as I discuss the dangers. He nods seriously, his respect for the creatures evident in his expression.

"Dad, are there any dolphins here?" he asks, his voice filled with curiosity.

I smile and shrug. "Possibly. The St. John River empties into the ocean, so it's not unusual to see a dolphin fin break the surface."

When he immediately scrambles to the edge of the boat, his eyes scanning the waves with a renewed purpose, I glance over at Anna. A smile flickers across her lips, mirroring my own amusement at his boundless enthusiasm. Our love for Connor creates a strong connection. Can we keep it to just a physical connection? Then, remembered past lies rear their ugly head like a warning, reminding me to guard my heart.

Eighteen

Anna

The boat ride was definitely a hit today. I smile as I glance down at Connor, who drifted off to sleep the moment his head touched the pillow. I lean over and place a soft kiss on his forehead, then turn to see Carson. The heat radiating from his eyes as I brush past him sends a current of electricity through me. My cheeks flush, and my breath catches in my throat.

I hear him whispering goodnight to our son as I go into my room to get ready for bed. Carson's offer echoing in my mind, I put on my cami and short set. I haven't given him an answer, mostly because I don't know how that change would affect Connor. A knot of worry tightens in my stomach. How would

Connor react if I moved into the master bedroom with Carson?

I sigh, as I've never been in this situation before. I've never been into the dating scene. A guy did invite me out two years ago, and when I suggested we meet at Starbucks for coffee while my son was at school, he suddenly bailed. I shake my head at the memory. Being a single mom can certainly be a detriment to dating. Not that it ever bothered me before.

I've never met anyone else who has called to me like Carson does. He's the only man I've ever truly been attracted to, but all these life changes are happening so fast.

I grimace as I know what I want to do. I crave the man's touch. If it were up to just me, I'd happily be in Carson's bed every night. But I have to consider my son... Maybe I should wait...

I hear the faint click of my bedroom doorknob being turned. I look up as Carson steps into my bedroom. At the lust-filled look in his eyes, it's suddenly hard to breathe. He slowly reaches out and then hungrily kisses my lips. I press myself against him, feeling his arousal. It makes me ache. He straightens and looks directly into my eyes. Seeing his own desire mirrored in mine, he bends and picks me up in his arms. Turning, he carries me to his bedroom.

He kicks the door shut. At my worried glance over his shoulder, he states huskily, "Connor's so dead to the world; even you screaming my name won't wake him."

He slowly sets me on my feet, letting me slide down his hard front. He steps back, and his eyes gleam down at me. He reaches out a finger and traces my white cotton camisole top. It's modest, but you couldn't tell from his gaze. He states in a soft whisper, "That night in the hallway, I could see the shadow of your nipples."

His finger slips from the edge of my cami, circling each nipple in turn through the thin cotton. They harden to stiff peaks at his light touch, and a shiver courses through me.

His hand continues to travel down to my shorts, to the curly scalloped piping around the leg openings. He runs his finger underneath the fabric, lightly caressing my thighs. He traces the outside, and then his hand moves between my legs, nudging my thighs apart. His searching finger grazes the juncture where my leg and torso meet—so close yet not touching that part of me that aches to be filled.

He suddenly reaches down, picks me up by my waist, and places me on his bed. I'm at the edge of the mattress; my legs hang over the side. He lifts my hips to slide off my shorts; next, he takes off my top. He quickly divests himself of his clothes and then kneels between my knees.

I feel his hot breath on that most intimate part of me. I clutch the sheets with my hands in anticipation of his touch. I look up to see his eyes devouring me as I lay spread before him. Instinctively, I try to pull my legs together. But his hands stop me and instead spread my thighs even wider apart to make room for his broad frame as he edges closer. He leans down and gives me a long, slow lick, and my hips almost come off the bed in response.

I hear his soft chuckle as he lifts one of my legs and places it over his shoulder. My hands tighten their hold on the sheet as he bends down and begins to pleasure me with his mouth. I gasp as his teeth lightly graze my clit. I suddenly let out the breath I've been unconsciously holding as my body gives in to the sensations he ignites in me.

When he inserts a thick finger, I gasp at the feeling. "Oh," I moan as he continues to prime me for what's to come. He pushes in another finger, and I tighten my leg around his back, pulling him in closer. My hands reach down and fist in his hair. I'm shamelessly holding him in place as my body begins to clench in response to his actions. He crooks his fingers inside me, and I swear I see stars as my body clamps down hard around him. He continues to work me even through my orgasm.

As I lay there spent, still spayed out before him, I realize my hands are still clutching his hair. I slowly loosen my hold and see him grin in the dim light. He stands and grabs my waist as if I weigh nothing at all, moving me farther up the bed. My head is near the pillows.

He follows, sliding between my legs. As I feel the tip of his cock probing me, I open to him. He surges into me, filling me with his thick, turgid length. He's big, and for a moment, I gasp because I'm still sore from the night before. He instantly stills. But I smile up at him, then reach up and kiss him. That's all the incentive he needs as he increases his strokes.

As the momentum builds, he begins pounding into me as we find that age-old rhythm that takes us toward the finish line. I can feel my orgasm as it builds. That faint tingle. I feel his hand reach down, and he firmly thrums my swollen clit. My body instantly responds, and for the second time tonight, I clench helplessly around him. I shout into his shoulder as I come hard while in his arms.

I hear his hoarse shout as he follows my bliss. His body is heavy, but I welcome it. He slides his weight to the side but keeps an arm tight around me. I snuggle into his side. Exhausted, I close my eyes and drift off to sleep.

When I open my eyes again, I'm in my own bed. The late morning sunlight streams through the window, and I realize with surprise that I've overslept. A smile spreads across my face as I realize Carson must have carried me back to my room. I slip on my robe and head for the bathroom, the sound of laughter filtering in from the living room.

Later, when I walk out my door, it sounds like cartoons are on. I hear Connor and Carson talking. "Cinamon Toast Crunch is okay. But let's face it. Cap'n Crunch has been around since before I was your age," Carson states.

Connor replies in an awed tone, "I didn't know it was that old."

I hear Carson snort with amusement. "Well, my cereal hasn't changed, but I can't say the same for cartoons. Why do they call him SquarePants?"

Connor explodes in a belly laugh, "I told you because he's a sponge!"

Peeking around the corner, I see Carson sitting in front of the television. Connor is sprawled on the floor beside him, both with bowls of cereal in front of them. The sight warms my heart.

Hearing their mingled laughter, I hate to interrupt. They have so many of the same mannerisms that it makes me smile—like father, like son.

I reach for my phone, a mischievous glint in my eye. This moment deserves to be captured.

It's Monday morning and I'm headed with Connor to his new school. "Did I already give you lunch money?"

"Nope. But Dad did," he shrugs.

"Oh, good. We went over the list, but I still feel like I've forgotten something," I say as I chew on my lip.

"It's okay, Mom. It can't be that important, or you would have brought it," Connor says with a maturity that surprises me.

I laugh, a sudden release of tension. "Who can argue with that logic?"

"We're here. That's the office." I point as we exit the car. A surprisingly short while later, after registering him for classes, I give Connor a side hug. I then walk back to the car and leave. The school and the staff seem very top-notch.

A glance at the clock assures me I have enough time to get home before the moving company arrives with our boxes. Carson made arrangements for some of our stuff to go into a storage unit at the apartment complex. He handed me the key this morning. It's a relief, as there are some boxes that I don't need on a day-to-day basis. I had the boxes already marked, so all I have to do is direct the movers where to put everything.

Right on time, I hear the doorbell ring.

It's hours later when a glance at the clock tells me it's almost time to pick up Connor.

As I leave the apartment, a sense of accomplishment washes over me. I have most of the boxes emptied and put away. The movers took everything else to the storage unit. The only thing left to do is break down the boxes, and Carson said we should put them in storage as well.

I haven't had time to learn the Jacksonville traffic patterns yet, but I manage to navigate the roads with surprising ease.

A glowing Connor comes running to the car when he leaves the school. "Hey, how was your first day?"

"Fine," he grins. "I like the teacher; she is nice. I also have a friend. His name is Jeff, like my friend Jeff in Lauderdale."

"That's great, Honey." Connor continues to describe his day as we head toward home. I surprise him with an ice cream stop to celebrate his first day at the new school.

As I drive to the apartment, a lump forms in my throat. Is now the right time to talk to Connor? This is uncharted waters. My heart races as I rehearse the conversation in my head a few times. How will he react? Will he be happy? Upset?

"So, Connor," I start hesitantly, "I um. I've been thinking... I mean... your dad and I..." I trail off, unsure how to proceed.

"Yeah, Mom?" He asks with a frown filled with confusion.

I smile and shake my head, postponing our talk for another time. "Not important. We better get upstairs."

Later that night, after Connor's in bed, I tiptoe out of my bedroom and into Carson's room. I'm naked under my robe. He's waiting for me in his bed.

After another round of sex, we lay tangled in the sheets. I lean over and trace the black tattoo across the right side of his chest.

"You didn't have this when we met on the cruise," I say softly.

He grins, "No, I got this a couple of years later. Do you like it?" He asks lazily.

"Very much, it makes you look like a badass," I tell him truthfully.

He chuckles as he pulls me on top of him. I lay my head on Carson's chest and listen to the soft thud of his heart beating. I yawn.

The next thing I know, I hear Connor as he yells, "Mom! ... Mom?" He yanks open the door to Carson's bedroom. He blinks in surprise at seeing me lying in bed with Carson. "There you are." He approaches the bed and grabs my hand. "Mom, come on, get up, or I'll be late for school."

"I'm sorry, Connor. I must have overslept." I try to act normal, "Get dressed, and I'll be out in a minute."

"Okay, but hurry," he warns with a small frown.

I get out of bed, slip on my robe, and look down at Carson. He's sitting up in bed with both hands behind his head, a huge smirk on his face. "I don't think our son has a problem with you sleeping in here," he says with a teasing glint in his eye, barely able to contain his mirth.

I roll my eyes at his words, "Yeah, I noticed that." I lean down to give him a quick kiss, and he grabs me and pulls me back into bed. "Guess this means you'll be moving in tonight. I'll make room in the closet," He says before he kisses me again.

Once I'm back on my feet, he delivers a slap to my ass as I walk away. "No excuses. I'll expect you in my bed every night," he says with a sly grin.

Nineteen

Carson

Sunlight streams through the picture window of my office. The view never gets old. I trace the familiar path of the river with my gaze. Its ceaseless flow mirrors the unexpected twists and turns my life has taken. I take a deep, calming breath, watching the gentle waves across the river's surface, a soothing counterpoint to the strange unease within me.

Anna. The thought of her sends a smile spreading across my face. I probably shouldn't have crossed that line, but instead of fading, the desire seems to intensify with every moment we're together.

I watch as a tugboat chugs by, the river's flow a constant reminder of life's ever-changing currents. Just like the river, my life has taken an unexpected turn, one that fills me with exhilaration and a sense of homecoming. But can I trust this feeling?

I groan when I glance at the clock. The board meeting with my brothers starts in minutes, yet here I sit, lost in my thoughts.

I stand up and stretch. This wasn't how things were supposed to be. Work used to be my life, my salvation. Now, it feels more like a chore, a distraction from the warmth that has filled my days since Anna and Connor arrived.

A month ago, work was the only thing that mattered. My life was stagnant. I was restless, yearning for something I couldn't define. Then Connor walked in, changing my life forever. He brought with him a whirlwind of energy and a love so deep that it scares me sometimes. I grin, just thinking of my son. He takes joy in the simplest of things.

And then there's his mother. I let out a sigh. I always come back to Anna. Between her and my son, my life has never been this full. They've brought a lightness back into my days, a zest for life that extends to every corner of my world. Now, I'm eager to get home and I'm learning to embrace the joy of the present moment, to savor the simple things – like eating breakfast together.

Suzanne knocks on my office door, snapping me back to reality. "Carson, it's time for the meeting."

"Thank you, Suzanne." I follow her across the hall to the conference room. Both of my brothers are already seated, amusement gleaming in their eyes.

"Sorry for the delay," I mutter, taking my seat. I turn toward Suzanne, "Could you read the minutes from the last meeting, please?"

She blinks, surprised by the request, "Of course." As she reads the minutes from the last board meeting, I nod along, but my mind is elsewhere.

"Ah, yes." I glance over at my brothers, who are grinning from ear to ear. "Okay, what's so damn funny?" I say with a stern frown in their direction. But I have a feeling I already know.

"Nothing, nothing at all," says Carter, but amusement lingers in his eyes.

Chase smirks and ever the blunt one states, "It's just that you used to eat, drink, and breathe work, and now—Well, now, you're like the rest of us. You're enjoying your life. It shows."

I try to glower at them, but I can't help but grin back. "Fine, I like having a family. More than I ever thought I would."

I turn to Suzanne. "The meeting's canceled. Why don't you take some extra time for lunch?" She nods with a happy smile and closes the door behind her with a soft click.

I rub my hand through my hair with a frown as I turn back to my brothers.

"Why the long face, Carson?" Carter asks me. Leaning back in my chair, I let out a sigh, "I'm not sure. It just feels surreal," I confess, "Four weeks ago, I didn't even know Connor existed. Now, we're living together like a family. I keep thinking I'll wake up one morning and find out it's just a dream."

My brothers exchange a knowing glance. Chase grins and says, "Carson. I get it. I was adamant I didn't want a child. Now, sometimes, when I look at Gabby, I break into a sweat, knowing I could have missed out on loving her. Val and Gabby are the best part of my life."

Carter gives me a considering look. "The last time we talked about Anna was at Wild Riders. I'm pretty sure circumstances have changed."

"Yes. We're sharing a bedroom." Both of my brothers just grin, their grins widen as Carter adds drily. "Well, that explains your good mood," he throws a wink in my direction. Then, suddenly serious, he asks, "Do you think there might be more there than you originally thought?"

I feel my jaw tighten, "It's too early to tell," I admit. "While we're compatible in so many ways, I can't let go of the past. She hurt me once, and I..." My voice cuts off. The memory surfaces, bringing with it a feeling of bitterness. "I wouldn't want to go through that again. Especially when we share a child." When I look up both brothers have a glint of understanding mixed with sympathy in their glances.

"Yeah, that would be tough," Chase readily agrees. "Just don't overanalyze things. If things are meant to be, then everything will work out." He shrugs.

"As you know, I tend to analyze everything," I admit with a rueful smile. "But I'll try to wait and see where this goes. Sometimes, it feels like we're a family, and then..." I hesitate, the weight of the past pressing down. "I remember old hurts." I don't want to discuss the details with them, feeling the need to protect Anna's privacy in some strange way.

There's a hesitant knock on the door. Chase jumps up and opens the door. I look up to see Anna standing in the doorway. "Sorry to interrupt. Clara, the receptionist, told me to come on up. She mentioned your admin was at lunch." She's dressed in black pants with a purple silk shirt that brings out the color of her eyes. Her chestnut hair falls in soft waves around her shoulders.

Chase's grin widens as the door swings open. "Hi, Anna," he greets, his voice warm. "We just finished up our meeting." He glances sideways at Carter, a silent exchange passing between them before he turns back to her. "We'll leave you two alone." With a nod in our direction, my brothers exit, the heavy oak door sighing shut behind them.

The silence that follows stretches between us. I clear my throat, the sound echoing in the sudden emptiness. "Did something bring you by, Anna?"

A blush creeps up her neck, painting her cheeks a pretty pink. "No, not really," she states with a hesitant smile. "I was in the area and thought I'd stop in. I haven't seen your offices before."

A slow smile spreads across my face. "Great," I respond, standing. "Let me show you around. Then we can go out to lunch if you'd like."

Her eyes light up with a smile. "That would be nice."

I lead her toward the door, the light scent of her perfume wafting around her. We descend in the elevator, the silence companionable. As the doors slide open on the ground floor, "This is where we train our security and bodyguard teams."

I give her a tour of the training grounds and the indoor shooting range. Once back in the elevator, we make our way to the first floor. "You've already seen the reception area. This floor houses most of our administrative departments. Human resources, accounting, and marketing." As we walk through the halls, I smile down at her, "Kat, Carter's fiancée, is the manager of our marketing department."

Anna returns my smile, a playful glint in her eyes. "Kat mentioned that," she says, her voice tinged with amusement. "She told me about a 'Bodyguard Calendar' promotion?"

I roll my eyes in mock exasperation. "Yeah, she tried to sweet talk Carter into participating, but he wasn't having any of it." My voice turns serious as I add, "Kat's definitely a force to be reckoned with in marketing."

Reaching for the doorknob, I usher her inside. "And this is my office," I announce with a touch of pride. The room is bathed in a warm glow, courtesy of the expansive windows. Her eyes light up as she sees the panoramic view of the river.

A gasp escapes Anna's lips. "Carson," she breathes, her voice laced with awe, "the view from here is breathtaking."

"I planned it that way," I reply with a self-satisfied smirk, "I'm the CEO, so I gave myself the best view and office."

Her gaze sweeps across the room, lingering on the dark wood furniture – a heavy desk, matching bookshelves overflowing with leather-bound books, and a comfortable round table with plush chairs. A surprised laugh bubbles up from her chest as she spots the discreet door tucked away in a corner. "You even have your own bathroom?"

With a hint of pride in my voice, I confirm, "Of course, and a personal coffee station right next to my admin's desk." I reach out, my fingers brushing against her arm before gently pulling her closer. The heat of her skin sends a spark through me.

"An admin who's currently out of the office," I murmur huskily.

Her breath hitches as I lean in, the scent of her perfume an intoxicating invitation. My lips graze the curve of her neck, sending shivers down her spine. Her eyes flutter shut, dark lashes resting on her flushed cheeks.

The world around us fades away as I claim her lips in a kiss. Her initial surprise melts into a soft sigh as she surrenders, her lips parting under mine. Our kiss deepens, a hungry exploration fueled by our desire.

I feel her shiver, and when she opens her eyes, they're dark with her arousal. I press her closer, her body molding against mine, the urgency building with every touch.

The sudden click of the outer door shatters the passionate world we've built. We both step apart, blinking in the harsh light of reality. I loosen my grip, my forehead resting against hers as we catch our breath.

A rueful smile curves my lips. "It seems I misspoke," I murmur. "Come on, let's get some lunch."

I walk out my open door, and Suzanne looks up startled, "Oh, sorry. I brought my lunch back to eat it at my desk. I didn't know you were with someone."

"Not a problem. Suzanne, this is Connor's mother, Anna Johnson," I introduce them, gesturing towards Anna. "And this is Suzanne Lion, my admin. She's been keeping Knight Security running smoothly for years."

Anna offers Suzanne a warm smile. "It's a pleasure to meet you."

"Likewise, Anna. Carson's a fantastic CEO and boss," Suzanne replies with a knowing smile in my direction.

Anna's smile widens. "I'm sure he is."

Once the elevator doors slide shut, offering a reprieve. Anna's gaze lifts to mine, a soft smile playing on her lips. "Even back then, when you talked about Knight Security, I knew you'd be a success. You had such a fierce passion for your family's business. I loved hearing you talk about your plans."

I nod, a flicker of surprise crossing my features. I hadn't realized she'd paid so much attention when I shared my goals for the company's future. I'm struck silent as I lead her to the parking garage.

The car's quiet is a comfortable silence. Pulling into a parking lot next to a brightly lit pub with a catchy sign—"Shot in the Dark" - I turn to Anna for her approval.

"This okay? They serve the typical bar food, but it always tastes great."

I lead the way into the high-end sports bar. "They also know me here. The co-owner, Jaxson, is a private investigator we work with often."

We settle into the red cushioned booth across from each other. After we've ordered, a calm silence descends as Anna lets her gaze drift around the sports bar. Large-screen TVs line the walls, muted broadcasts flickering silently. I catch her eye and gesture toward a small control panel on the table. "Each booth has its own volume control," I explain.

She leans forward to curiously look at the control panel with a small smile. She seems as content as I am with the sound muted. The low murmur of conversation and the clinking of glasses create a soothing atmosphere.

As Anna drains the last sip of her white wine, a satisfied sigh escapes her lips, "That was good," she murmurs, setting down the empty glass. "And the food was delicious."

I signal for the check, feeling pleasantly full. Suddenly, a familiar voice cuts through the air. "Carson! Good to see you." A tall, broad-shouldered figure walks up to our table, a welcoming grin spreading across his face. "How's business?"

"Jaxson," I greet, returning his smile. "Things are good. This is Anna Johnson," I introduce, the words feeling a little stiff on my tongue. "An... old acquaintance." A mental groan escapes me as the words leave my mouth, entirely inadequate for the complex history we share.

Jaxson's grin falters for a moment before he recovers smoothly. "Nice to meet you, Anna," he extends a hand as his eyes swivel between us with a hint of curiosity. "I don't think I've ever met one of Carson's acquaintances before. I hope you enjoyed your lunch?"

Anna responds with a tight smile that doesn't quite reach her eyes. "It was excellent. Thank you," she replies with a brittle laugh.

Twenty

Anna

The silence on the drive back to Knight Security is profound. Neither of us attempt to speak. I mean, what did I expect him to say? I close my eyes wearily.

As soon as Carson turns off the car, I open the passenger door and jump out. As I head to my car, Carson tries to stop me. "Anna! Listen." But I don't slow my steps, and I don't turn around. Once I'm in my car, I immediately start the engine, wanting to avoid a conversation, but Carson approaches my window. I take a deep breath, and then, with reluctance, I hit the button to roll it down. I refuse to make this easier for him.

I sit there staring straight ahead. When he doesn't say anything, I finally cut my eyes to his. "You're more than an acquaintance, and you know it. Words just failed me there for a minute."

I nod without responding. He finally spreads his hands and says, "I'm sorry. Okay?"

"Thank you for the apology, Carson." He winces at my icy tone.

As he goes to turn away, I state, "An acquaintance? Really?" I give him a tight smile that doesn't quite reach my eyes, "You could have just introduced me as your friend, Carson."

He freezes, then slowly leans down toward the window and reaches in to turn my chin toward him. In a deadly quiet voice, he states, "You and I have never been friends, Anna."

With those parting words, he stalks away. After he's gone, I blink back the tears that well in my eyes, hot and stinging. I put the car in drive and pull out into the Jacksonville city traffic. About a block down the road, the tears spill over and silently roll unchecked down my cheeks. I feel their dampness as they soak into my silk shirt, but I don't care. I let them fall.

By the time I enter the apartment, my tears have dried, leaving behind a numbness. I grimace, remembering one of Carson and Connor's favorite songs, Pink Floyd's Comfortably

Numb. That's exactly how I feel. Instead of going to the master bedroom, I'm drawn to the spare bedroom. A sense of foreboding snakes through my body.

I know I hurt Carson all those years ago, but he's the one who wouldn't listen. He never even gave me a chance to explain.

I sit down in the small armchair as I think back... to when I discovered I carried Carson's child. I felt numb then, too, but it didn't last long. When a doctor confirmed my pregnancy, the news came as a physical shock. Once the numbness finally left, it opened the door to a flurry of emotions – fear, excitement, and a gnawing worry about Carson. I knew I had to tell him, but a cold knot of dread coiled in my stomach.

Picking up my phone, I hit his number, my heart hammering against my ribs. Then, I realized Carson had blocked my calls when they went directly to his voicemail. I stammered out a message. Asking him to call me. I didn't hint at why, just that I needed to speak with him. He never returned any of my calls.

I went to Graham's bedside. It was one of his rare good days. He was sitting up in bed and gave me a gentle smile when I entered.

"Anna, are you alright? My dear child, you look like somebody who just lost their best friend," he said in a voice that held his concern.

I sat down on the side of the bed, reached over, and took his frail hand in mine. I looked down, seeing his parchment-like skin, showing his dark veins. The chemotherapy treatments had not been kind. He looked so white against the sterile sheets.

"Graham, I'm pregnant," I admitted in a low voice.

He nodded and squeezed my hand, "I take it the father, is the young hot head from the cruise?"

I gave a small laugh at his accurate depiction of Carson. "Yes," I admitted with a sigh.

"Anna, I'm so sorry that I put you in this situation," he said in a sorrowful voice.

"Graham, you did no such thing. You offered me financial freedom," I assured him in a fond voice.

"Only so you could care for me," he pointed out ruefully.

"I would have taken care of you no matter what. You're the only family I've got."

The unconditional love that shined out of his eyes had my eyes watering. "So, if you decide to marry this man, I could contact my lawyer. I'm sure we could get an annulment."

A flicker of hope flared in my chest, but it was quickly extinguished as I remembered Carson's final goodbye. "Thank you, Graham. But, I... I don't think he'd listen to me right now."

"Anna, from what you've told me of him, he may be a hot head, but there had to be something redeemable about him for you to fall in love with him," his gentle voice held a note of admonishment.

"There was," I admit to him. "I just don't know how to get through to him." I adjusted some of the tubes that went from his weakened body to the machine's beeping plaintively in the corner. "Besides, who would take care of you?"

"I have plenty of money; I could hire someone," he assured me stubbornly.

"But, I want to take care of you, Graham. Don't you know that?" I said, tears coming to my eyes.

He reached out and wiped the one lone tear that escaped. "Please, don't cry, Annie, or you'll have me blubbering like an old fool, as well."

I smiled at the childhood nickname. "Graham, I'm worried that even knowing I'm having his baby won't make a difference in how Carson feels." I finally hiccup through my sniffles. The baby hormones seemed to be already making me even more emotional.

"Poppycock," Graham muttered. "He can't be that unforgiving. If he is, he doesn't deserve you."

His words felt like a balm for my wounded heart. "Thank you, Graham. I can always count on you to be my champion."

"Of course you can. You know, I only insisted we marry to ensure you receive my inheritance. If it wasn't for Neal..."

"Graham, we've been over this. I won't leave you. Ever. Even if Carson did come around, he probably wouldn't understand that I want to care for you," I said in a firm voice.

"My Anna, I think my stubbornness is rubbing off on you." A sudden fit of coughing wracked Graham's already frail body. Panic surged through me as I scrambled to grab his medication.

When he finally stopped coughing and leaned back against his pillows, he patted the empty space beside him. I moved closer and gave him a hug, being careful of the medical tubing. His weak arms went around me, and he patted the back of my head,

"In that case. I'll leave everything as is. But if the time should ever come." I tried to stop his flow of words, "No, Anna, I mean it. If you ever need to be released from our agreement. I will make sure it's done."

"I know, Graham. That means a lot," I said softly. He then patted my head to comfort me, like the time as a child I scraped my knee. "Annie, it's going to be alright. At least I'll die knowing you and your child are taken care of." I didn't protest because we both knew the cancer would eventually take him.

After Connor was born, I helped Graham hold him. He took such delight in watching Connor grow from an infant into a toddler. It was almost three years to the day before Graham passed away quietly in his sleep. I was inconsolable at first, feeling all alone.

When Connor crawled into my lap, his tiny hand instinctively reached for my tear-streaked cheek. I held him close, the warmth of his small body a welcomed comfort against the emptiness I felt. Connor was too young to understand the loss, but his presence offered a sweet hope for the future, a future I had to build for both of us.

Connor was too young and doesn't truly remember Graham, but I hope he can recall the love that he lavished on both of us.

My phone buzzes beside me, and I blink my eyes. It's the alarm I set up as a reminder so I wouldn't miss picking up Connor. I look down at my tear-stained silk shirt, knowing I have to change it before I leave.

I wearily pull myself out of the armchair. My heart is heavy with remembered grief. I miss Graham. I once teased him that only the good die young, and he gave me a weak smile and said, "That's why I've made it to seventy-two."

I shake my head at the fond memory and pick up my keys on the way out the door.

At the school, my gaze fixes on Connor as he shuffles towards the car. Instead of his energetic gait, he advances with sluggish steps. His face looks pale, lacking its usual healthy color.

"Hey, Baby. Is everything alright?"

He shrugs, "I dunno," he mumbles as he leans his head back against the seat. "I don't feel so good," he says in a voice barely above a whisper.

Worry knotting in my stomach, I immediately reach over to feel his forehead. "You're burning up. Did you tell your teacher or the school nurse?"

"No, I thought I'd get feeling better," he says, his lips turning down in a frown. "But I don't."

"Let's get you home," I say as he buckles his seat belt.

Once we enter the apartment, I suggest quietly, "Why don't you lay down for a little while?"

When Connor just nods his head and does as I suggest without protest, I know he's feeling bad.

He changes into his sleep clothes and then crawls between the cool sheets. I approach with a thermometer, and he dutifully opens his mouth.

"Doesn't anything hurt, Baby? Your tummy or your chest?"

"My chest hurts sometimes," he mumbles.

"When does it hurt?" I probe for details.

"When I take a deep breath," he gulps in some air and then starts coughing.

I frown as his cough sounds raspy. "Let me call the doctor."

I call my doctor in Ft. Lauderdale and speak with a nurse practitioner. After answering all their questions, she advises, "I would treat him for a cold or flu. However, If the rattle in his chest gets worse, you'll need to get him to a doctor. He may have walking pneumonia and need antibiotics."

I tell her thank you and disconnect the call.

I reach out and touch his forehead. It's still hot and dry. "Okay, Baby. You rest here. I'll be right back."

I search the apartment for any type of cold and cough medicine. Right as I'm about to give up, I find a container with liquid medicine that I can give him for now.

After Connor is sleeping peacefully, I text Carson, letting him know that Connor is sick. Then, I give him a list of things to pick up on his way home.

While I wait for Carson to respond to my text, I wearily sit down on the bed, a worried frown on my face as I lovingly watch my son as he sleeps.

When my phone finally buzzes, I glance down at the text and read, 'I'll be home by five; let me know if you need anything else. Take care of our boy.'

I give a relieved smile. No matter how Carson feels about me, I know he loves Connor and will always be there for him.

I sigh as I reach out and gently brush Connor's hair back from his warm forehead. It's hard being a single parent, especially when things like this happen.

I carefully lay down on the bed beside Connor and watch the gentle rise and fall of his chest in a comforting rhythm. Despite the worry gnawing at me, a flicker of gratitude warms my heart.

I'm not alone in this.

Twenty-One

Carson

When I enter the apartment with a bag filled with the items from the list Anna sent me to pick up, silence greets me. I quietly place the bag on the counter and then make my way to Connor's room.

The door stands open. A sliver of light from the hallway illuminates the room, revealing Connor nestled under the covers, his brow furrowed slightly. Anna lies beside him, one hand resting gently on his chest, her breathing soft and even. They are both sound asleep. I give a gentle smile at the touching sight that tugs at my heartstrings – they both look so vulnerable.

I quietly leave without waking them, closing the door softly behind me.

I rummage through the bag, finding the medicine Anna had requested. Years of bachelorhood have left me ill-equipped on how to care for a sick child. A strange mix of protectiveness and resentment stews within me. It feels good to be needed, to be doing something for Connor, yet the reminder of my absence from so many years of his life stings. I wasn't the one to pick him up when he fell, to put a band-aid on a scraped knee. So, many years missed.

I glance around the kitchen; I've gotten used to dinner being ready when I get home. Knowing Anna won't feel like cooking, I scroll through options. Finally, deciding which food delivery sounds the most tempting for them, I call it in.

Feeling satisfied that I've done what I can. I head to my bedroom to change out of my work clothes. Emerging later in jeans and a T-shirt, I go to the kitchen.

After years of capably living alone, I'm suddenly at a loss without Anna or Connor around. I frown at the mixed emotions coursing through me.

A sigh escapes me as I sit down at the kitchen counter. A pang of guilt goes through me as the image of Anna's stricken face haunts me. My words were cruel, a knee-jerk reaction fueled by years of simmering resentment.

The real truth is— Anna means a lot to me. Just thinking about her sends a thrilling pulse through my heart. But friends? No, we've never been friends. My feelings for her are too volatile. They're a mix of pure primal lust along with an undeniable attraction that I could never ignore.

I crave her body too much for me ever to try and disguise those feelings under the mantle of friendship. Being her friend would be an impossible act; I am too irresistibly drawn to her.

I grimace because instead of conveying that to her, I allowed her to think the worst. Shame burns in my throat, a bitter aftertaste to the harsh words that tumbled out. I squeeze my eyes shut, the memory of Anna's wounded expression sending a fresh wave of remorse through me.

I run my hand through my hair in frustration. We're locked in a stalemate. Even if I could find it in my heart to forgive her deception, the trust I once had in her is irrevocably gone.

I rub my face with the heels of my hands. It's a no-win situation, a maze with no exit. I trust her with Connor, the most precious thing in my life, but entrusting her with my heart feels like I'm walking on eggshells. One false step and everything could shatter.

The buzz of my phone pulls me from my chaotic thoughts. It's a text that our delivery has arrived. Not wanting to disturb their slumber, I step into the hall to wait for our food.

When I re-enter with dinner, the apartment door clicks shut behind me. I watch as Anna shuffles into the kitchen. She rubs the sleep from her eyes, yet they still show signs of stress.

"Dinner's here," I announce as I lift the bags onto the table. "I ordered Italian."

She nods her thanks and then goes straight to the medicine I purchased. "Is Connor okay? What did the doctor say?" I ask with a concerned frown between my brows.

Anna states quietly, "I spoke with the nurse practitioner at our doctor's office in Ft. Lauderdale." She brings me up to speed on what was advised. "So, do they think there's a good chance it could be pneumonia?" I ask as a knot of worry starts to tighten in my gut.

"Only if the rattle in his chest worsens," she states matter-of-factly, with only a slight concern. I get the sense that she's been through this before.

"I understand. Um... Would you like to eat? I ordered Italian, Connor's favorite." I manage to ask her as she turns around, a few of the bottles of medicine in her hands. "Yes, but later." Then she's gone.

I hear hushed voices, so I move to his bedroom and stand in the doorway.

Connor lies snuggled up in bed. He's awake. His cheeks are flushed a feverish red, and his normally bright eyes are dull.

Anna rubs ointment on his chest, which has a strong medicinal spell. She tucks in the covers as he rests against the pillows.

Anna leans in closer, her voice dropping to a soft murmur, a soothing melody meant only for Connor's ears. She tucks a stray strand of hair behind his ear, a gesture filled with tenderness. I watch as she carefully measures out the medicine and helps him raise the cup to his lips.

"Make sure you swallow all of it, Baby. It's cherry flavored, and you like cherries," she advises gently.

As Connor hesitates, she states, "It will make you feel better." He swallows all of it, but he still grimaces once it's gone. "That's it," she says.

The silence is broken only by Connor's labored breathing and Anna's hushed reassurances. I linger in the doorway, a silent observer of this intimate scene.

A lump forms in my throat as I watch Anna care for our son. My presence feels almost like an intrusion, yet a part of me wants to be closer, to offer comfort to Connor, and to help lift the burden of responsibility off Anna. I shift my weight as I stand hovering in the doorway.

Anna glances behind her and sees me. She then looks down at Connor and asks gently, "Do you feel like eating something? Your dad brought dinner. I have a feeling it's spaghetti and meatballs."

For the first time, Conner's eyes brighten, "My favorite? Okay," a rasp to his voice.

I step forward, "Hey, Son. Heard you aren't feeling well." Connor offers a weak nod, his usual endless energy dampened. I walk over to him and ruffle his hair, and he doesn't even try to duck his head. "I'll get your dinner."

I come back with all three containers. We all sit on the bed and eat together—a temporary truce between Anna and me.

A flicker of his usual grin returns as he eats his spaghetti. Connor doesn't eat that much. Yet, every bite that he finishes is a small victory against how lousy he feels.

Once we've finished the meal, Connor yawns, and his eyes start to droop. Anna and I pick up the containers and quietly exit his room. We leave his door open.

Her shoulders are tense, and her back ramrods straight as she carries the dinner trays into the kitchen. She glanced at me briefly, a flicker of something unreadable crossing her features.

She finally turns and walks over to the medicine again. "I'll need to find a local doctor," she turns slightly toward me, "Then I'll have Connor's medical records transferred."

"If you'd like, I can ask around for references—" I begin, but Anna quickly shakes her head. "No, I'd rather ask a few of the other parents from his school."

"Fine. Whatever you think is best," I say quietly, unsure how to bridge the chasm my earlier words created. I reach out a hand to gently touch her arm. "Anna..." I start, but she turns away, and my hand falls to my side.

She crosses her arms and turns her back to me, clearly a dismissal.

Shit. Now, what do I do? I probably deserve her cold shoulder treatment, but I don't like it. Not one bit. And I won't put up with it for long. But I know I hurt her. So, for now, I'll give her some space.

"I have some errands to run. I probably won't be back until late," I say in a chipped voice. "If you or Connor need anything, just let me know."

She again nods without turning around. With a frustrated frown and anger at myself for causing this tension between us, I head for the door.

When I get to the parking garage, I take one look at my SUV and decide I'm in the mood for something faster—a ride that matches my reckless mood. I throw the cover off my motorcycle, revealing the gleaming chrome of my Harley. Without a second thought, I hop on and gun the engine. The deep rumble is a welcome sound that helps to dispel the turmoil within me.

As I pull out onto the city street, the amplified roar of the engine seems to mirror my emotions. When I reach the open highway, I increase my speed. The rush of the wind in my hair feels good, and I feel my black mood start to lift.

When I pull into Wild Riders, I look around in surprise that I chose this destination, as I hadn't consciously planned on stopping anywhere.

I nod to the regulars that congregate in the front but don't stop to talk. I walk through the heavy oak doors. The place is usually bustling, but tonight is a weeknight, and it doesn't look that busy. I glance at the booths but then head straight for the bar. As I slide onto a stool, Spitfire, with his red bandana around his biceps, approaches. "Draft?"

"Yes, thanks." As he sets an icy mug down in front of me, "My uncle around?"

"Yeah, Shadows in back. Want me to get him?"

"Nah, If I don't see him by the time I finish this, I'll find him." Spitfire nods and then turns to pour a drink for a customer at the other end of the counter. I sit there nursing my beer as I listen to the bar sounds around me. The low murmur of voices, with the occasional burst of laughter, and behind it all is the sound of pool balls as they clack together from the other room.

I feel a pat on the back, "What brings you in tonight?" I glance sideways as my uncle slides onto the neighboring barstool.

"Just felt like a ride and ended up here." I give a noncommittal shrug, but the tightness in my shoulders and the forced casualness in my voice betray my churning emotions.

"Humph." The sound comes out of Sam's mouth as his eyes narrow on me.

My uncle motions to Spitfire, who sets down a draft in front of him. "So, how are things at home?" He asks casually. I take a deep breath, then admit, "Connor's in bed with a cold. Anna's taking care of him."

A knowing glint enters my uncle's eyes as he offers a slow, deliberate nod. "Ah, I see," he rumbles, his voice laced with a quiet understanding that puts me at ease. He takes another sip of his beer, "That's normally when your dad would come around here."

I raise my brows at him, "Really?"

He grins and gives me a look from under his bushy eyebrows, "Yep. He said he always felt helpless when one of you boys got sick. He said he felt like he was in the way." I nod in agreement. "Your mother normally knew what to do. But you know, Bonnie relied on your dad to be there for her. She said it was a shared responsibility raising you three boys."

We sip our beers silently for a few minutes—no words needed. Then my uncle glances back at me and says with a considering look, "The other times your dad would drop by is when he and Bonnie had a fight. He used to come here to clear his head."

I glance over at my uncle and give a sheepish smile, then just nod and take another sip of my beer. Sam continues, "It was normally some foolish thing he had said that hurt her feelings. Guys can be plumb stupid when it comes to communicating with women." He nods his head sagely.

I glance over at him again, "Then what would Dad do?" Sam smirks, "Well, your dad was a bit of a hot head. Like you." He gives me a nudge, "But, he'd come here to cool off and think things through. Then, after one or two beers, he'd head home." Sam glances over at me with a wink, "He'd say he was sorry and give her a kiss." He shrugs, "Always seemed to work for your dad."

I pick up my glass and drain it. Then I throw a twenty on the bar and turn to my uncle. "Thanks." He chuckles and states, "That's what uncles and bars are for."

Twenty-Two

Anna

It's late, and I'm sitting in the armchair watching Connor sleep. He looks so young and helpless when he's like this.

I lean my head back against the wide armchair. I snuggle into it and get more comfortable. I wrap my arms around my legs and pull them against my chest. It's late, and I'd rather be in bed, but I'm worried because Carson isn't back yet. I sigh. I hate feeling this tension between us, but I don't know if I'm ready to forgive him just yet.

I feel the hot sting of tears again, but I refuse to let them fall. Instead, I throw fuel on the fire of my anger as I mutter mockingly, "Besides, I'm not even his friend. No. I'm just an acquaintance…"

He already apologized, and the logical part of me whispers, *how should he have introduced you? 'Hi, this is Anna, my date.' No, we're not dating. 'My girlfriend.'* I grimace. *'This is Anna, my lover, the mother of my child, whom I just discovered I had. Oh, what you hadn't heard?'* I shake my head and roll my eyes at my silly internal dialog. But it's helped soothe my hurt feelings and appeased my anger.

The other reason I haven't gone to bed is that I don't know if I should sleep in the master bedroom when things are so unsettled. Should I sleep in the spare room? Won't that reinforce the wall between us? If I'm honest, I'd rather fall asleep in Carson's arms than alone in the spare bedroom… I snuggle deeper into the armchair.

I wake up as strong arms, warm and familiar, envelope me before I can even register what is happening. My eyelids flutter open, seeing Carson's face close to mine as he scoops me up and gently holds me to his chest. He carries me into the master bedroom, shuts the door, then lays me carefully on the bed.

Seeing I'm awake, he softly takes my hand in his, "Anna. I'm sorry. I should have told you… the reason I could never be your friend... is because you are, and have always been, way more than a friend. I desire you too much."

He squeezes my hand and then gives me an earnest look, "I feel many emotions when we're together, but being friendly is not one of them." He takes a deep breath and then says, "As for being my acquaintance - I know I already apologized for that, but I wasn't prepared to introduce you to someone who didn't know about Connor." He looks directly into my eyes so I can see the sincerity in his eyes.

Carson's words flow over me like a wave, washing away the hurt and leaving behind a glimmer of something precious... a fragile hope for our future.

He gently brushes the back of my hand with his lips. Even that soft touch makes me shiver. His eyes start to gleam, and he leans forward and gives me a sweet kiss.

At least it starts out as sweet. When I raise my arms to pull him down against me, the kiss deepens. Then, as always, just one touch and that small flame of desire is soon a raging inferno.

Suddenly, there are too many barriers between us; we're both desperate to be naked. He's pulling my shirt over my head, and I'm trying to pull off his T-shirt. Next, my hands fumble to unbutton his jeans. We help each other as our clothes fly off and land around the room. Until, finally, it's just bare skin against bare skin. Then he lands on the bed beside me and urgently pulls me on top of him.

"Ride me, Anna," he whispers hoarsely as he grips my hips and helps position me above him. I lower myself onto his hardness inch by inch until I'm fully seated. We both gasp in satisfaction at the intimate connection.

Then I start to rock against him. I go in a circular motion, slow and steady, and I hear him give a low groan. I throw my head back and feel my long hair cascade down my back.

Carson's hands reach up and cover my breasts. He fondles them as I continue to move above him. When he lets out another groan, I grin at him. He makes me feel so wanton, so... womanly. Knowing I can bring him to this sexual level is intoxicating. I half close my eyes as I deliberately increase the pace, wanting him to lose control.

As I again move in a circular motion against him, he rasps, "Anna... Baby. That feels so fucking good."

I purposely slow the pace as I make the same motion again. "You're killing me," he grinds out. Then I feel his broad hands as he grips my hips, wanting me to go faster.

"It's only what you deserve." I taunt him with a teasing smile. His hands suddenly tighten, and he rolls until I'm on my back, and then he's on top of me. My startled eyes meet his.

"This is what you deserve," he says gruffly as I feel his cock surge into me. Then, neither of us can speak as he continues to stroke into me. We both shout out as bliss takes us, and he empties himself into me. As I lay their spent, Carson gets out of bed and strides naked into the bathroom.

When he comes back, he has a warm washcloth and slowly cleans me. "Carson, you don't have to—" He cuts me off with a soft kiss. "I want to," he says gruffly, "You take good care of us, Anna. It's about time someone takes care of you." I'm left speechless at his words. The sincerity in his eye sends a warm feeling flowing through me.

Once he's done, he takes the washcloth back into the bathroom and stops to open our bedroom door wide.

After he crawls back into bed, he pulls me closer. I snuggle up against him. There's a huge smile on my face because I know Carson left the door open so we could hear if Connor needs us during the night.

That open door feels like a symbol of our newfound unity, a silent promise that we can face whatever comes next together.

The dim light filtering in from the hallway casts long shadows on the wall, but within the circle of Carson's arms, I feel safe, secure, and cared for.

The rest of the week goes by in a blur as Connor's health improves. By the weekend, he's feeling bored, restless, and ready to climb the walls. We've watched movies and played cards as well as video games.

We hear the front door open, and we look up in surprise as Carson walks in. "You're home early," I say with a look of surprise. Connor jumps up and runs to the door. "Hey, Son. It looks like you're feeling better," Carson says with a pleased grin.

"I am... but Mom won't let me do anything," Connor mumbles with a pout. "I've been cooped up in here all day. It's boring!"

Carson laughs, but I roll my eyes. "Yes, he's bored, and I'm feeling the strain of trying to keep an energetic ten-year-old entertained for hours on end," I admit.

"Well, if your mother thinks it's a good idea. I thought, maybe, we could go fishing." Both sets of eyes turn toward me. "What do you think, Anna? It isn't too strenuous. It would get Connor outside..." As I hesitate, he adds, "And out of your hair. Besides, you need a break."

"It sounds perfect for all of us," I say, giving Carson an appreciative look. Connor whoops and runs to his bedroom. Then he comes back out with a frown on his face. "What do you wear when you fish?"

Carson grins and says, "I'm wearing shorts and a T-shirt."

I smile a mile wide when both of them reappear, matched similarly in navy blue shorts and white T-shirts. They look so much alike that I get a lump in my throat. "Here, I hand Carson a small cooler filled with ice and cans of soda. I also give him a bag filled with snacks, and I warn him, "Connor's got his appetite back."

Carson gives me a brief kiss while Connor hugs me goodbye. The door shuts behind them, and silence settles over the apartment, a balm to my frayed nerves. I look around the empty apartment, and my grin blossoms into a wide smile.

It's later when I glance at the clock with a feeling of satisfaction. The afternoon has flown by, and I've made good use of my time. I've soaked in a hot bubble bath, painted my nails, and read a few chapters on my e-reader of the latest romance book. A surprise dessert sits in the fridge, and I have a casserole bubbling in the oven, awaiting their return.

After spending the afternoon fishing, they enter the apartment, grinning from ear to ear. "Did you catch anything?" I ask with raised eyebrows. "Yes!" Connor practically shouts, his face beaming with excitement. He launches into a detailed account of their shared afternoon, punctuated by dramatic hand gestures to show the size of the fish.

Carson and I exchange a glance over Connor's head, sharing a grin at our son's unrestrained enthusiasm. "Then we released them back into the water, and they swam away."

Carson, a proud smile, tugging at his lips. "Connor did great out there. He even caught twice as many fish as I did!"

A wide grin splits my son's face, his eyes sparkling with delight at his accomplishment and his father's praise.

Carson states, "We stored the gear in the storage room. So, it's ready for next time." He takes in a deep breath and glances into the kitchen. "What do you have cooking? It smells amazing!"

Connor rubs his stomach as he lifts his nose in the air to take a whiff, "Yeah, it does. I'm starving."

I smile as I inform them, "It's Chicken Tetrazzini. I'll get it out of the oven while you guys wash up."

When they return, we all gather around the table while the aroma of the delicious food continues to fill the air. Connor's laughter rings clear, speaking volumes of his recovery. The flush of vitality shows on his cheeks, and his eyes sparkle with mischief from their fishing escapade.

A wave of warmth floods through me as I witness the joy unfolding before my eyes. Leaning back, I let a quiet smile curl my lips, basking in the glow of their enthusiasm. As Connor entertains us with tales of their shared afternoon, each chuckle, each glance, stitches our family fabric tighter. It's a moment that paints a hopeful picture for our future—bright yet fragile.

After we've finished dinner, they both help clear the table. "Why don't you guys pick out a movie while I put the dishes in the dishwasher?"

Connor eagerly bounds toward the living room, with Carson following him more slowly. After loading the dishwasher, I serve the decadent dessert and carry the plates to the living room.

"Who wants dessert?" I ask with a grin. Two sets of eyes widen in surprise. "I do!" Connor yells immediately, while Carson just holds out his hand for the plate. I give him his serving and then get Connor settled so there's less chance of a spill. As they take their first bite, I wait to see how they like it.

"Mom! This is great! I love cherries!" While Carson states, less vocally but with obvious appreciation, "Damn. This is delicious, Anna."

I do a mock curtsy, "Thank you. It's called Cherry Delight. Graham cracker crust, cream cheese filling, and cherries." I tick off the ingredients as they dig in. "It's been quite a while since I made this. In fact, the last time I made this, I was…" My words suddenly trail off, and they both look at me with identically raised eyebrows. I shrug, "Sorry. I… lost my train of thought. It's been so long that I don't remember when I last made this dessert." I say with a self-deprecating grimace and a shrug.

Connor pipes up, "Dad, can we watch the movie now?" Carson hits the play button, and I sit back as the action movie scrolls across the screen, but my mind is elsewhere.

Twenty-Three

Carson

The manila envelope feels almost heavy in my hands, its weight far exceeding the few sheets of paper it contains. My fingers trace the embossed lettering of my lawyer's firm, a wave of satisfaction running through me as I contemplate the contents within.

With a deep breath, I open the envelope with an equal mixture of anticipation and relief. A satisfied smile tugs at the corners of my lips as I scan the contents.

Inside is Connor's updated birth certificate, and I couldn't feel more pleased and proud.

My lawyer handled filing the petition to establish paternity and Connor's name change. It took a while, but now, legally, Connor is recognized as my son and bears my name.

I lean back in my chair and rub my chin. Now, how do we publicly announce this? While I want to shout it from the rooftops, I probably need a more dignified way to get the word out. I pick up the phone and buzz Kat. "Kat, do you have time to drop by my office this afternoon?"

"Of course, Carson. I'm free right now if that works?"

"That works perfectly. Thank you."

I buzz Suzanne, "I'm expecting Kat for a brief meeting. Can you send her in when she arrives?

"Certainly. Do you want me to bring in any refreshments?" Suzanne, who is always efficient, asks me.

"Iced tea would be nice. Thanks, Suzanne."

I look up with a smile when Kat walks in. "Hi, thanks for meeting me on such short notice."

She gives me a curious look as she takes a seat in front of my desk. I hand her the manilla envelope as Suzanne arrives with the glasses of iced tea and sets them down. "Thank you," I murmur before my admin closes the door behind her.

I take a sip of the tea as I watch her intently, searching for a reaction as she unfolds the document. A bright smile blooms on her face, and she looks up at me with a sparkle in her eyes. "Congratulations, Carson. It's now official."

I nod and say with a hopeful look, "Yes. I was hoping you might have a few suggestions for the best way to announce that I have a son."

Kat nods thoughtfully, and I can tell she's already mulling over a few options in her head. "I have a few questions. Do you want to announce it, go big and splashy publicly? Or do you want to get the word out quietly?"

I frown as I consider her questions. "I would prefer to get the word out quietly."

Her brow creases in concentration, and she drums her fingers with thought. "You're constantly getting asked for interviews. What if we agreed to have a couple of interviews?"

Kat stands and paces as she thinks of the different options, "One with the local paper and another with a national magazine, possibly Billionaire Tech. When they ask you about your personal life, you'll mention you have a son, Connor. That would get the news out publicly as well as locally." She turns to me with an inquiring look.

"I like that idea," I admit readily.

"There's a chance this could snowball," Kat cautions, her voice laced with concern. "This could be picked up by a gossip rag and sensationalized. But then again," she shrugs, "they could do that anyway, regardless of these interviews."

"True, so there's no reason not to go forward," I reason.

She smiles again. "I'll set up the interviews. In the meantime, why don't you guys go ahead with the Knight family cookout? Let your friends and the rest of the family know."

"Sure, we can do that. Maybe later this month." I nod.

"Also, you have that ground-breaking ceremony for the new charity. I think you should take Connor. Have him stand beside you during the photo shoot," Kat continues, "Take him along for any community events you have scheduled."

"Kat, thank you. These are all good suggestions." I tell her with a sincere smile.

"Anytime, Carson. That's what families do," she says with a teasing grin, "Besides, handling marketing and publicity is what you pay me for." Kat stands and walks to the door, then she turns. "One final question, Carson. Forgive me for prying, but what about Anna?"

I cock an eyebrow at her, "What do you mean? I'm not sure what you're asking?"

Kat bites her lip, then states carefully, as she searches for the right words, "If we're going to be introducing your son," she begins, her voice softer than usual, "it might also be a good opportunity to clarify your intentions or relationship with..." she faltered for a moment, "Connor's mother."

I frown at her words. "I would rather leave Anna out of this," I say, my voice hardening. Let's focus solely on my son."

Kat's eyes widen at my harsh tone, her glance filled with silent questions, "Understood. I'll get those interviews scheduled... if you should change your mind—"

"I won't," I say in a chipped voice.

Kat nods slowly, her expression unreadable for a moment. "Absolutely," she finally says, her voice regaining its usual professionalism. "Just making sure all our bases are covered. I'm on it, Carson."

I try to shake off the pang of guilt that washes over me as Kat leaves my office. But right now, I need to make arrangements for Connor to accompany me over the next month. I buzz Suzanne, "Could you come into my office and bring my schedule for the next sixty days?"

I leave work early and stride eagerly into the apartment. "Anna? Connor? Anybody home?" My voice raised.

They each jump up from their spots in the living room, their faces mirroring each other's curiosity. Smiles tug at the corners of their lips, hesitant yet curious as they approach. My throat tightens as I reach out, holding the manila envelope like a precious treasure.

Anna's smile falters for a breath before blossoming into a radiant grin. With a trembling hand, she takes the envelope and reads the updated birth certificate. A soft gasp escapes her lips as she looks from Connor to me, and her eyes well up, threatening to spill over.

Ignoring the sudden lump in my throat, I kneel before Connor. My hands land on his small shoulders, and his gaze meets mine, wide and searching. I try to speak firmly, but my voice betrays me, a tremor underlying the words, "You're officially part of the Knight family now, Connor Carlton Knight."

The fierce hug that follows steals my breath. I hold him close, the warmth of his small body a comfort. When I finally release him, his face is flushed, a suspicious glint in his wet eyes. "I'm a Knight now!" he declares, his voice thick with a newfound pride.

Suddenly, he turns into a whirlwind of excited energy, bouncing around the living room with unleashed enthusiasm. He continues his antics until I say loudly, "Let's celebrate! Where do you want to go, Connor?"

He skids to a halt in front of me, his eyes shining. "Main Event!" He blurts out, a grin plastered across his face. "They have laser tag!"

My wide grin mirrors his. "Main Event it is, then," I chuckle, ruffling his hair. As I pull him into one last squeeze, my eyes meet Anna's over his head. Her gaze holds a loving tenderness that sends a wave of intense emotion through me. Overwhelmed with the rush of feelings, I reach out an arm, silently inviting her into our hug.

A watery smile graces her lips, and she sinks down beside me. We hold each other close in a warm embrace, sharing a silent yet poignant moment of joy.

The Main Event is a huge arcade-type building that houses laser tag, bowling lanes, and more games than I've seen before.

We follow Connor as he's a blur of energy, ricocheting from one game to the next. The reward tickets pour out of the machines in a triumphant clang. He collects them carefully, already searching for the next challenge.

Connor and I play our first game of laser tag. It's a battlefield as I dive behind a neon-lit pillar. Connor launches his attacks, a gleeful shriek escaping his lips. The kid's good, I grin with pride. Anna meanwhile opted to play skeet ball, adding to Connor's growing pile of tickets.

We head to the dining area and order our dinner. Anna gets iced tea while I order a draft beer. After the first bite of my cheeseburger, I look up, and my surprise is evident. "Wow, this is actually pretty good," I admit before taking another savory mouthful.

Anna's lips curve into a knowing smile. She leans in, her voice a conspiratorial whisper. "It's a far cry from Chucky Cheese," she confides, "that used to be his go-to celebration spot."

I shudder, just thinking of greasy pizza and sticky floors. "Let's just say," I deadpan, "I'm starting to appreciate this place a whole lot more. We both watch with a touch of amusement as Connor hurriedly gulps down his food, not wanting to miss a minute of fun.

As the night draws to an end, Connor again heads toward the laser tag section, wanting to squeeze in one more game. Anna agrees to join us this time.

As they gear us up and explain the rules, I glance at Anna. She has her long chestnut hair tied up in a high ponytail. She's wearing curve-hugging jeans and a halter top that shows off the bronze glow of her shoulders. The excitement that shines from her eyes makes her look younger than her age. She holds the laser in her hands like a pro.

Connor and I are on the same team this time, and she's on the opposing team. We're with a larger group of teenagers, and we all look eager to start. As we enter the darkened space, the neon structures glow in the black lighting. Someone shouts, "Game on!" and we all scatter and begin shooting.

Connor stalks around, landing a few good shots. His hair falls over his eyes as he takes aim at another opponent.

I suddenly get hit and jerk my focus back to the game at hand. I try to shoot back in defense, but my laser has to recharge when I'm hit again. I look up, already planning my retaliation, as I see Anna shielded behind a neon-bright window.

I duck and maneuver until I'm coming up behind her. Then, I strategically take my shot. It hits her, and her vest flashes as her laser has to recharge. As I go to set up the next shot, in a surprisingly agile move, she ducks behind a form and disappears. I advance steadily. I see others on her team, but I ignore them as I evade their lasers. I'm on the hunt for Anna.

I spot Connor as he raises his arm in a triumphant gesture and lets up a whoop after taking down another opponent. Then I spy Anna. She's got her back to a wall, and she's glancing over her shoulder at someone on my team. As she's solely focused on aiming, I silently approach her.

Right after she shoots, I make my move. Instead of taking my clear shot, I reach out and push her back against the wall. My lips find hers in the darkness, and I push hungrily into her mouth as I press my weight against her. When I finally raise my head, my body has hardened, and I hear her take in a raspy breath. I grin smugly down at her, feeling arrogantly pleased when I see her clear gray eyes are now cloudy with desire.

My eyes watch her as she turns her face up to mine with a sweet smile. Suddenly, my vest starts to flash brightly, indicating I've taken a direct hit. I frown down in shock, then notice that her laser gun is still pointed directly at my vest. She shot me!

With a wicked grin, she steps back, turns, and runs. I follow her in swift pursuit.

Twenty-Four

Anna

When we finally left the Main Event, it was late. Connor held the prizes from his tickets against his chest as if they were treasures. His tired but content grin made the night of fun a worthy celebration.

The heat smoldering in Carson's eyes made the rest of the evening feel like foreplay. The lights blinked on when he caught me, and the laser game abruptly ended. Ever since that moment, there's been a promise of retribution in his eyes that had me catching my breath in anticipation.

Carson is tucking Connor in. Our son was sound asleep when I left him. I shiver racks my body as I get ready for bed. Remembering the hot look in Carson's eyes, I dressed for bed in a daring black lace teddy. When I hear him enter the bedroom, I step boldly out of the bathroom.

His eyes flare when he sees what I'm wearing. His gaze feels scorching as it rakes over my form. He quickly divests himself of his clothes and then turns toward me, his eager cock already at full staff as it stands proud against his stomach.

Carson's eyes narrow as he demands in a gruff voice, "Come closer, Anna." Another shiver courses through me as I slowly approach him. His eyes gleam with appreciation and lust as he studies my breasts through the provocative black lace. It hides nothing from his view. I feel my nipples pebble just from his gaze. I swallow thickly.

"You're a wicked temptress, Anna." His words are hot against my cheek as he leans in closer. I left my hair down, and it now falls in waves around my shoulders.

One eyebrow arches as I sink to my knees in front of him. I reach out and boldly wrap my hand around his engorged cock. I fist him and slowly stroke from root to tip. I hear him take in a ragged breath of air as I lean forward and softly blow across the tip. There's a drop of precum, and I daintily give it a lick.

I feel his hands as they roughly settle into my hair as he pulls me roughly forward. I open my lips to take his hardness into my mouth. His hips surge into me as he purposefully strokes in and out.

I continue to work him with my mouth and my hands as I lightly caress his balls. I can tell he's close to losing control as he continues to pump between my lips. "I love to watch your lips as you take my cock into your mouth," he says in a guttural tone. His hands in my hair tighten as his strokes become more aggressive.

Just as I deep-throat him, ready to take all he has to offer, he pulls my hair roughly, stopping me. "Wait," he commands in a hoarse mutter. "I want to come inside you." I blink up at him from the sudden interruption.

"Get on the bed," following his demand, I turn around. At his harsh intake of breath, I smile, knowing he's just noticed that my panties are a thong.

I crawl onto the mattress on all fours. He crawls onto the bed and positions himself behind me. I feel his blunt fingers as he slowly pushes aside the thong; his fingers continue to glide into my folds, probing my slick wetness. "You're wet for me," he says hoarsely.

Then I feel his hard grip on each hip right before he surges into me. His thrust is so powerful I fall face forward into the sheet. I quickly brace myself with my arms as there's no stopping him. Like a freight train, he plows into me again and again. I rise up to meet his thrusts; the sex is wild and rough, and it's such a turn-on.

I feel the tingle of my orgasm as it builds inside me. He must feel it, too, as he backs off on his thrusts. Slowing his pace while I pant in frustration. I was so close.

My legs quiver from my exertion in this position. He reaches for a pillow and shoves it under my belly. Then he begins to thrust again. If possible, he feels even harder, longer as he slams into me. My stomach muscles clench hard from the rough claiming of my body. He grunts as he continues to pound into me. I'm again close, and he again deliberately slows.

I whimper helplessly as my orgasm fades. "Carson, please," I practically beg him to let me climax. "I thought you liked playing games, Anna." He taunts me through gritted teeth. "Yes, but I'm... I'm so close. Carson, please!"

He leans forward over me as he whispers in my ear, "Who's in control here, Anna?"

I remain silent, not wanting to answer him. I push back against him, urging him on. He ignores my movements. "Anna, who controls your body?" He demands again.

When I don't answer him, he grinds out, "Who controls you? Say it," he orders me roughly.

I open my mouth, helpless against his demands, "You do." I finally admit in surrender, desperate for him to continue.

At my agreement, he forcefully thrust into me, and my climax again starts to build.

"Now, Anna. Come now." He commands me hoarsely through gritted teeth. His palm stings as it makes contact in a hard smack against my ass cheek. At the slap, my entire body clenches uncontrollably as I'm finally allowed to climax, and I shout out his name as I come hard.

I feel his body climax with me, and he emits a low groan. Then, the weight of his heavy body leans against me, and my arms collapse. We both fall against the bed. Spent. He rolls to his side, taking me with him. All my energy is gone. I feel his arms pull me until he's curled around my back. Exhausted, I close my eyes and let sleep take me.

When I wake in the morning, I'm alone in the bed. I reach over, and the other side of the bed is cool. Carson's been up for a while. There's a beam of sunlight showing between the blinds. I've overslept.

I give a lazy stretch. I glance down, and I'm still wearing my lingerie from the night before. Seeing the black lace against my skin, I feel a surge of womanly satisfaction. A secret smile plays on my lips, and I remember Carson's reaction when he saw me wearing it.

I crawl out of bed and then listen at the door. I smile when I hear Connor's boisterous laughter. And in the background, there is the sound of funny cartoon characters. I smile as I remember it's Saturday morning. Knowing I have no reason to hurry. I head for the shower.

When I finally leave the bedroom, I'm fully dressed in crisp white shorts and a black-and-white striped shirt that shows off my figure. I brush my hair until it gleamed with a healthy shine. It now cascades loosely around my shoulders. Not knowing of any plans for today, I put on a light coat of mascara to accentuate my eyes but otherwise left my face clean of makeup.

I enter the living room and see Connor sprawled in front of the television, his now empty bowl of cereal in front of him. I lean down and pick up the bowl. "Morning, kiddo," I say as I pat him on the head. "Where's your dad?"

Without his eyes leaving the screen, he answers, "He went to get his laptop out of the car."

"Has he eaten breakfast?" I ask Connor, "Yeah," he answers between his giggles at the characters dancing across the screen.

I place his bowl and spoon in the sink alongside Carson's empty bowl. I fix a bagel for myself and grab the cream cheese from the fridge. I put on a kettle to have a hot cup of tea. I'm sitting at the kitchen counter, just about to bite into my bagel, when I heard the front door open. I glance over my shoulder. Carson enters with a briefcase in his hand.

His eyebrow raises as he surveys me, sitting there at the counter. The glimmer in his eyes has a wave of warmth flooding my cheeks. He places his laptop on the table and comes up behind me. He leans down and whispers for my ears only, "I seem to remember you glancing back at me like that last night, too." Then he slides my hair behind my shoulder and brushes his lips across my cheek.

As he stands, he spies my bagel. "I see you like a little bagel with your cream cheese," he says in a teasing tone, his amused smile tugging at his lips.

I look down and then give him an answering grin. "Yes, I do." I then take a bite, relishing the taste of the warm toasted bagel smothered under a thick layer of cream cheese. With a slow sweep of my tongue, I catch any leftover bits of cream cheese. A satisfied sigh escapes my lips. I continue until every crumb has disappeared from the plate.

Carson powers up his laptop and sits down in front of it. When the kettle goes off he looks up with a curious look. "I made tea. Would you like a cup?" I ask as I stand and walk toward the kettle.

He frowns as he shakes his head. "No, but I wouldn't mind another cup of coffee."

I pour the steaming water over my tea bag and let it steep. Then I grab the coffee pot and fill his empty cup. As I place it in front of him, his arm goes around my hips, and he gives me a brief side hug.

I get my hot tea, add some honey, and bring the fragrant brew with me as I sit down across the table from him. While I sip my tea, my eyes study Carson as he pulls something up on his computer. His chiseled jaw has a shadow because he hasn't shaved. His dark hair hangs over his forehead, and I want to brush it back with my fingers. But I don't disturb him. I'm content with just looking for now. I sigh; I could easily look at him all day.

The silence stretches comfortably between us. Cartoons play in the background while sunlight filters into the dining room through the wide picture window.

Feeling my silent scrutiny, his eyes dart to mine. "I talked to Kat about the best way to introduce Connor as my son. She suggested he attend some of my more public community appearances."

I nod with a soft smile, "Good." I finish my sip of tea, "He may need a suit or at least a few more dress pants and shirts."

Carson smiles, "Yeah, most of these are pretty informal. There's a ground-breaking ceremony next week and other things like that. But there's a formal event at the end of the month. He'll need a suit or tux, and you'll need a formal gown."

"Okay," I murmur, mentally going over my wardrobe. Carson then throws out, "My mother and the girls know a place. I doubt if they would have a tux for Connor, though."

"That's fine. Let me know where you got your tux, and I'll take him shopping."

Carson continues, "I'm sending you a copy of my schedule. My admin has the events with Connor clearly marked."

I grin as I suggest, "You'll need to instruct him on how to behave—and, more importantly—what not to do in front of the cameras." I offer with a twinkle in my eye.

"Understood. My father was at a similar event at a construction site when I was young," Carson chuckles as he tells the story. "The photographer was delayed. By the time he arrived, I was covered in dirt from head to toe."

"Like father like son," I murmur as I shake my head fondly. Carson nods, "I'll be sure to explain that if he's bored, he needs to let me know. I'll gladly pay someone to keep him looking presentable."

I frown, slightly confused, "Pay someone? I promise to keep him out of trouble."

Carson glances at me, an unreadable look in his eyes. "Anna, I thought it would be best if you... avoided being in the public eye, for now." He gives a casual shrug. "Until this whole thing blows over. Kat said the gossip rags could get ahold of the story and blow it out of proportion."

A hesitant nod is about all I can manage to his casually spoken words. Each one feels like a slap in the face. No, worse, like a dismissal, a rejection of our relationship. I try to shove down my initial reaction, but my chest aches, a dull pain that spreads through my limbs. What does this mean for us? Does he not view us as a couple? Confusion and hurt swirls in my mind, a tangled mess of mixed emotions.

Twenty-Five

Carson

The Florida sun is turning the ground-breaking ceremony into a personal sauna. Sweat trickles down my back, soaking into my starched white dress shirt. I shift uncomfortably from the growing dampness that clings to my skin.

It's a ground-breaking ceremony, but the publicity coordinator felt it would be more dramatic for us to cut a ribbon instead of throwing a shovel of dirt. I don't quite get her logic, but I'm only here as a representative of Knight Security. Our company has contributed money and resources to this particular charity.

Next to me, Connor mirrors my stance. A wide grin plastered on his face. He doesn't seem to mind the heat, his youthful energy never wilting. While I feel a simmering frustration. This ribbon-cutting charade, while dramatic, feels like a colossal waste of time.

Finally, they announce, "Okay, you can begin to cut the ribbon." Connor, with a huge grin on his face, eagerly plunges the oversized scissors down with a flourish. I offer a grin when I'm directed by the photographer. The cut ribbon flutters to the ground as the watching crowd gives a rousing cheer.

Connor and I swiftly step out of the way as people surge into the space: the publicity coordinator and the photographer approach. "Hey, your son is a natural. Those photos I got with his smile will go over big." I reach down and squeeze Connor's shoulder in praise.

The coordinator leans down and states, "Hear that? Your picture is going to be in the newspaper and on the evening news tonight."

Connor just shrugs like it's no big deal. I hide my grin as I ask, "Are we done here? Have you gotten all the pictures you need?" The photographer assures me, "Don't worry, I got plenty. Thanks for your patience, both of you."

With that, I shake their hands. As I usher Connor away from the crowd, I glance down at him. "I don't know about you, but I'm ready for lunch."

Connor replies with a grin spread across his face, "Me, too! I'm starving!"

I smile as I shake my head, as my son always seems to be needing food. As we climb into the air-conditioned car, I steal a glance at him. "What kind of food sounds good?"

He scrunches up his nose in thought. "I don't care. How about Chick-fil-A?"

"Perfect." I put the car in gear and drive toward the fast-food restaurant.

Once we've stuffed ourselves with chicken sandwiches and waffle fries, we make our way to the car. My mind wanders to thoughts of Anna as Connor keeps up a constant chatter on the drive home.

I shift uneasily in my seat as I remember how she looked this morning when we left. Her smile was brittle and didn't reach her eyes. She never said a word to me about my decision to keep her out of the public eye. But I can tell that my words hurt her. She acts like nothing is wrong, but the easy-going camaraderie that was developing between us seems to have evaporated.

I can't say I regret my words, but I didn't tell her the entire truth. It was also for her protection. When Kat mentioned the gossip rags, my first concern was for Anna. I didn't want some fame-hungry reporter splashing gold-digger all over the media. Her sordid history needs to remain in the past - where it belongs. I feel adamant about that.

We step into the elevator, I hit the button, and the doors close.

Connor looks over and, with a grin on his face, asks, "Dad, do you know why the number six is scared of the number seven?" I think about it for a minute, knowing this is a joke, "No, Connor, why is six scared of seven?" Connor's eyes are filled with merriment as he gives the punchline, "Because seven ate nine!" I can't help it. I break into a grin and then start to chuckle along with him, and soon, we're both laughing hardily as we enter the apartment.

I know the minute I smell something simmering on the stove, I messed up. Anna avoided me this morning as Connor and I got ready to leave. I never got a chance to tell her about my plans to grab lunch before we came home.

Anna comes around the corner. "Welcome back. I hope you're both hungry." The smile on her face appears forced. "I made spaghetti and meatballs with plenty of garlic bread."

As Connor and I glance at each other with guilty expressions, her eyes narrow in suspicion.

Giving her my best apologetic smile, I mutter, "It's my fault. We stopped at Chik-fila on the way home."

As her face tightens, I try to smooth things over, "Sorry, I should have mentioned it when we left this morning." At her continued silence, I say a bit defensively, "I didn't expect you to go to all this trouble for lunch."

I watch as she takes a deep breath. "That's fine. I understand." She walks into the kitchen and turns off the stove. Over her shoulder, she says to Connor, "You should probably change out of those clothes before you get them dirty." A sharpness to her voice that isn't normally there.

Connor wisely nods, turns, and, with a sheepish look in my direction, escapes to his room.

I watch as Anna, her shoulders stiff and her back ramrod straight, begins pulling down food containers from the cabinets. She dishes a small portion into a bowl for herself and then methodically starts transferring the remaining food into containers.

I stand there for a few frustrated moments but she studiously keeps her back to me. "Anna, it was just fast food, but I should have called to let you know." At her continued silence, I feel like a heel. I walk into the bedroom, peel the sweaty dress shirt over my head, and drop it in the hamper with a grimace. I take a quick shower, then change into jeans and a T-shirt.

When I emerge from the bedroom. "Where's Connor?"

"He's taking a shower," she mutters, about the same time my mind registers the sound of running water coming from the main bathroom.

I guess I was expecting Anna to be over the lunch misunderstanding. She isn't. She avoids my eyes as I step farther into the room. I immediately go on the defensive. "Really? You're still angry because I took Connor to lunch?"

She swirls around and then places her hands on her hips. "You could have mentioned it this morning." She flings at me.

I fire back, "You were avoiding me!"

Her chin rises in a defiant gesture. "You could have texted me," she says, her tone icy.

I nod, "Yes, I could have, but I forgot." I then mutter, "I already said I was sorry. What else do you want? Blood?"

She turns wounded eyes toward me, "That's unfair, and you know it." She stammers in a shaky voice.

I take a deep breath, trying to control my temper. "Look, we both know this goes deeper than a missed lunch." I tell her in a hard voice, "You just need to trust me. I'm doing everything for the right reasons." There's now a sharp edge to my voice as well.

At my words, her eyes go wide in outrage, "I need to trust that you're doing it for the right reasons?" Her voice is cutting, "When you can't trust me at all? You won't even let me tell you about my marriage. Let alone talk about Graham—"

"Stop! Not another word." I ruthlessly cut off her communication. "I don't want to hear about your marriage or your late husband," I say with a sneer.

"Carson, if you'll just let me explain—" I hear the pleading in her voice, but I clench my jaw and shake my head. "No, Anna. Not in my house. I don't ever want to hear one word spoken about *him*." I grit my teeth as I refuse even to speak his name. The words I tossed down are like a challenge as I stand my ground.

I watch Anna, her throat working as she gulps in a few hurried breaths. She closes her eyes, and when she opens them, they are swimming in tears. I refuse to let her tears sway me. She finally nods in defeat. We both hear the main shower turn off. Anna hurries into the master bathroom.

When she emerges sometime later, her tears have dried. But the stress lines around her eyes only appear deeper.

I shrug off my guilt at the sorrow I saw in her eyes earlier. I push it firmly down as I try to convince myself that I have the right to demand she not speak his name. But deep down, I know that I'm being unreasonable in my request. Yet, I stubbornly don't change my mind.

A week's gone by, and it's again the weekend. We're driving over to my mother's for the family cookout. Anna brought her Cherry Delight dessert at Connor's insistence.

My son sits in the back of the car, his eyes wide in anticipation of the family gathering. "These cookouts," he asks, leaning forward in his seat, "they started with your dad, right? My grandpa?"

He's asked me to tell him about the cookouts. "Yes, Carlton Knight, the man you're named after." I have to clear the huskiness from my voice before I go on.

"He loved to entertain as much as my mother. Every four months or so, he'd throw a big hog roast and invite everyone he knew. It soon became legendary." I say with a bit of laughter in my voice. "After my dad died, the cookouts stopped for years. When your Uncle Chase married Val, she said your grandma might be lonely. So, we started having the cookouts again."

Connor pipes up, "And you had to buy a new cooker, right?" I grin, as he's heard the story many times but never grows tired of it. "Right, a new smoker." Then I continue as I promise, "Today, you'll get to meet all sorts of family. There's going to be a huge crowd."

The car engine clicks off, and I hop out. I grab the door for Anna as she carefully balances the sweet dessert.

I take her hand, and we weave through the people who have arrived. The air is filled with the smoky scent of grilling meat. It's a picture-perfect day—the sky is flawless blue, with not a single cloud in sight.

My brothers and I had tarps strung up to provide shade from the relentless Florida sun. The soothing sound of the nearby river provides a constant soundtrack as the backyard fills with a mixture of happy chatter and laughter.

My brothers and I man the grill and smoker. While tables groan under the heavy weight of the numerous covered dishes that promise a multitude of different tasty bites. While kegs of beer and overflowing ice chests offer cool refreshments.

There are several boats already docked, and their owners are expertly securing them to the wooden pier. The huge boathouse stands as a silent sentinel, watching over the scene.

I scan the crowd, searching for Connor. A smile spreads across my face as I spot him by the river, playing with a group of kids. He's met more family members today than he ever imagined possible. His eyes widen with wonder as everyone takes turns introducing him to the entire Knight clan. When Anna tries to hang back, I take her hand firmly and include her in the introductions to my family and friends. Her delighted smile was my reward.

Jaxson greets us with a hug for Connor and a grin for Anna. He throws me a quizzical glance. "Acquaintance, huh? I get it. I guess you weren't ready to explain about your son." He pats me on the back heartily. Turning, he introduces Anna to his wife, Maggie, a vibrant redhead with sparkling green eyes. He picks up their daughter, Mandy, a toddler with Maggie's red hair and his own dark eyes. She waves shyly, then hides her face in her father's shoulder.

My family welcomes Connor with open arms. Every single one of them embraces him with a welcoming hug. The old-timers, those who remember me as a child, declare the resemblance "uncanny." To them, the three of us are a family, even without a ring on Anna's finger.

My eyes follow Anna as she makes her way through the dwindling crowd. She's wearing a blue flowy sundress that swirls around her legs, and the bright sunlight makes her chestnut hair gleam.

If my family and friend's speculative glances bother Anna, she doesn't let it show. I give a deep frown. She's been quiet lately, not her usual cheery self. At first, I thought I might have irrevocably broken the fragile bond that had started to form between us with my outburst that she not talk about the past. But there's no outward resentment, no simmering anger directed at me. No, this runs deeper. A silent worry seems to follow her like a cloud.

Living together, spending time together..., and sharing stolen moments throughout the day have only reinforced my attraction to her.

She gives a zest to my life that wasn't there before. She's so easy to be around. Never one to hold a grudge, she's sunshine to my grumpiness. Her soft smiles and gentle touches have me racing to get home at the end of the day.

They also leave me craving more from her. I've tried hard to keep her at a distance because I can't erase the past. But another part of me aches for a deeper connection, a hint of the spark I saw in her eyes so many years ago.

A heavy sigh escapes me as I realize the truth—the truth I've been hiding. I'm in danger of falling in love with Anna, and it terrifies me. It could shatter the world as I know it, leaving me with only torn fragments of my once-guarded heart.

Twenty-Six

Anna

Late afternoon shadows dance through the leaves. It's been a wonderful day filled with family, laughter, and an endless stream of introductions. Connor has certainly enjoyed himself.

I settle into a chair across the table from Val and Kat, feeling pleasantly tired. "Where's Gabby?"

"I put her down for a nap," Val confesses with a fond smile.

I sigh as I lean back in my chair. "Girls, I am officially beat," I say with a sheepish smile. "And there is absolutely no way I will ever remember everyone's names."

They both give a tinkling laugh. Kat rolls her eyes, and Val just shakes her head. Leaning forward, Val confesses, "We don't remember half their names either. But there are so many Knights it could take years." Val glances over her shoulder at her mother-in-law, "I don't know how Bonnie remembers them all."

Kat looks over at me, a flicker of satisfaction in her gaze. "Carson seemed happy to introduce you to everyone," she says.

I nod as I agree, "I noticed that myself." A small smile spreads across my face.

Kat gently probes, "So, everything is going well between you two?"

I shrug, feeling a slight pang of unease flutter in my chest. "I guess as well as it can."

Val pulls herself up off the chair. "Anybody want anything? I swear this is my last trip to the dessert table." Her dimples flash.

Kat answers, her eyes twinkling, "I'll take anything with chocolate. I'm not picky."

Val laughs and then looks at me. I cave and say, "If there's any more of that Cherry Delight I brought, please bring some for me." As she goes to turn away, "Or anything with cream cheese!"

Val's steps falter for just a moment, a funny look on her face. She then makes her way to the dessert table. Kat and I continue to talk about the different family members we've met.

Val's back with cheesecake for herself and a chocolate brownie for Kat. She turns to me, a large helping of Cherry Delight on the paper plate. "That's the last of your dessert," she says with a smile.

She sits down across from me, and we all dig in. As I greedily lick the last bit of dessert off my spoon, I sigh. "I could have eaten the entire dish." Val and Kat look equally satisfied as they clean their plates.

I feel Val's eyes on me as I wipe my lips with a napkin, a speculative look in their depths. She glances around to make sure no one's listening. "Anna, you know when we were discussing our pregnancy cravings..." Her eyes go from my now empty plate to me. "You said you had an insatiable craving for cream cheese..." She lets the words trail off, but her eyes study me keenly, searching for a reaction.

I feel my face lose all color, the blood rushing from my head. I'm suddenly at a loss for words. I lick my lips and then look down at my plate. Tell-tale color then floods my pale face. I look up, "I forgot I told you that," my voice barely above a whisper.

Two sets of wide eyes stare back at me, then flicker to each other in silent communication. Kat is the first to reach out, her hand warm and reassuring on mine. "We won't say anything. Will we, Val?"

Val nodded solemnly. "Not a word."

I take a deep, shaky breath, forcing myself to calm down. I lean forward, I confess in a hushed tone. "I haven't confirmed it. I haven't even taken a home test. But the signs all indicate..." My words stop as I give a brittle laugh, "I can't get enough cream cheese, and I'm so emotional. I've always been irregular, but—" My gaze darts between them, seeking solace. "I have a doctor's appointment next week."

Val leans forward, her concern evident. "Has Carson noticed?"

I shake my head, "No, like I said, I'm very irregular, and I haven't had morning sickness."

"That's a blessing, at least," Val says with a sympathetic glance.

Kat asks quietly, "Are you happy about this? I ask because, well, you seem a little... sad."

I give a wavering smile, "I'm happy, truly. It's just that I don't know how Carson will feel. I don't know if he wants a future...

with me." I glance over at them with a sorrowful smile, "I've hurt him in the past..." I glance away, my eyes unfocused.

When I look back at them, I murmur, "I don't want to go over past mistakes. But I don't know if Carson could ever love me..." Again, my voice trails off. I give a rueful smile as I shrug. I briefly close my eyes, and when I open them, they are filled with determination. "And I would never force Carson into something he doesn't want." There's a finality to my words.

Kat states with a dry smile, "Well, it's not like you got into this condition by yourself. He can't blame you. He's equally responsible." Val nods her head in agreement.

A sudden wave of gratitude washes over me. "Girls, thank you. I mean it. It feels good to have you two as friends." They both lean in to give me a huge hug, their embrace a silent promise of support.

With a deliberate switch in topic, we chat about lighthearted things as the sun dips further down the horizon. Its rays cast long shadows when we scrape back our chairs and stand. The smoky scent of the grill lingers in the air, a reminder of the day's festivities.

Bonnie approaches us, her voice warm. "We have a cleaning crew coming. They should be here in fifteen minutes. We only need to handle any leftover food. They, thankfully, will take care of the rest."

We follow her over to the guys as they transfer any remaining barbecue into large aluminum foil trays. There's enough meat that Bonnie insists we each take home a tray.

Goodbyes are exchanged. Val and Kat give me meaningful looks as they hug me goodbye. We all pile into the car and head home. Connor is quiet in the back seat. Carson glances in the rearview mirror and then grins over at me. "He's practically asleep." I nod. "I could drift off myself," I admit sheepishly.

Carson's warm, answering smile is a sign of satisfaction. "He's now part of the Knight clan," he murmurs. My smile falters at his words, but his eyes are on the road, so he doesn't notice.

That night, Carson makes slow, sweet love to me. Afterward, we fall asleep in each other's arms.

Doctor's offices everywhere have the same medicinal smell and vibe. This one is no different. I chose to go to a general practitioner, but I know deep down what the blood test will reveal. This morning, my breasts were tender, and I felt slightly nauseous until I ate another bagel smothered in cream cheese. You'd think that would upset my stomach, but instead, it settles it down. It was the same when I carried Connor.

I wipe my sweaty palms on my jeans, the thin denim offering little comfort. Right then, they call my name. "Anna Johnson?" I stand and follow the nurse to the back.

Now, I'm sitting on the examination table. "You're here as a new patient. You came in for a regular check-up?" she confirms as her eyes scan the form in front of her. I nod, then say, "Yes," as her eyes haven't left the screen. Her eyes finally cut to me with a friendly gaze. " Is there anything else we should know?"

I lick my lips, the action automatic, before forcing out the words, "There's a possibility I could be pregnant."

At my admission, the nurse simply nods. "This states you're currently taking birth control pills; is that correct?"

"Yes," I admit, clearing my throat. "I called my nurse practitioner, and she called in a prescription here locally." I quickly stammer the next part in a rush, "I called her the day after we…" My voice trails off, a faint blush on my cheeks.

The nurse gives a curt nod. "I'll make a note of that." She busies herself with the computer once more, tapping away at the keyboard. "Alright, let's get your blood drawn. The doctor will be with you shortly."

She leaves me sitting in the cold room wearing a paper gown. The first nurse already took my blood pressure. When she said it seemed a little high, I explained I was nervous because of the visit. She just gave me an impersonal nod as she jotted something down.

I sigh and then hop down when I spot a magazine lying on the counter. I carry it back as I climb onto the examination table and then skim the pages and pictures. My mind is too filled with conflicting emotions to want to read an entire article.

Finally, I hear a light knock, and then the door opens. It's an older male doctor with graying hair and faded blue eyes, but his smile is warm. "Hello, I'm Dr. Simon," he says as he holds out his hand. His palm feels warm against my colder one.

He approaches with an old-fashioned clipboard. He sets it down and then listens to my heart as I take a deep breath as instructed. "Your blood pressure seemed a little high when we compared it to your records. but the nurse said you were nervous?" He asks that as a question. So, I answer him. "Yes, a little." He looks down at the clipboard again. "You're single with a ten-year-old child?" I nod quietly, fidgeting in the paper gown, the coarse material prickling my skin as I wait for his next words.

"Well, you're still young and healthy. The blood test did confirm you're pregnant." He stops as I absorb his words. They leave me feeling numb. But really, I already knew I was pregnant, so I shouldn't feel so stunned.

"Did you have any difficulties with your first pregnancy?" He inquires.

"No," There's a dullness to my answer. He looks up sharply, "Were you hoping for other news?"

With a soft smile, I assure him, "No, doctor. Not at all." I place my hand protectively over my abdomen. I already cherish this child." His eyes shine at my words, and he gives an approving smile. "In that case, I'll recommend an OB-GYN, but since your iron is a little low, I'll go ahead and prescribe some prenatal vitamins."

After he leaves, I methodically remove the paper gown and put on my clothes. I quietly leave the room and follow the exit signs to the front.

The woman at the counter says, "Congratulations, Mrs. Johnson. Here's a written prescription. You can have this filled anywhere." She then goes over the papers and pamphlets she has for me. She puts everything in a bag and hands it to me. I pay, and when I turn to leave, she states in a cheery voice, "Have a great day." I paste on a smile. "Same to you, thanks."

Once I'm in the car, the engine off, I grip the bag tightly. I sit there for a good ten minutes, and each second seems like an hour. Finally, I power on the engine and drive back to the apartment.

A knot forms in my stomach as I wonder what I should do with the pamphlets the doctor gave me. Connor constantly forages through the car's glove compartment, so leaving them in the car is out of the question. I can't take them into the house. I don't want them found, and I don't want to throw them away. I remember Carson gave me a key to the storage room.

I pick up the bag, walk through the garage parking lot, and unlock the storage room door. I hesitate about which box to put them in. Then I see the bright yellow box filled with Graham's stuff. It's perfect. I lift the lid and put the bag of pamphlets inside, keeping only the papers I need. I fold those and place them inside my purse.

I take the elevator up to the apartment. I'm not yet ready to discuss this with Carson. I decide to bide my time and tell him once the moment is right. My lips twist in a cynical smile as I wonder if there will ever be a right time to tell him.

That night, we gather in the living room with popcorn bowls in front of us. The movie is good, but the emotional scenes tug at my heartstrings, and my eyes fill with tears. I try to discreetly grab a tissue from the box sitting on the end table.

Carson catches my movements and grins, his eyes soft. He leans over and gently wipes the tears from my eyes. Then kisses me on my nose, and my eyes fill with tears again. "Hey, are you okay?" He asks in a low voice.

"Yes," I hiccup. "It's just... the movie," I explain, my voice thick with emotion.

He grins. "I know, women cry at movies." He puts his arm around my shoulders and leans me into him. His hand rubbing up and down my arm in a soothing gesture. I swing my legs up on the couch as I lean into his warmth. The weight of the secret I carry becomes a heavy burden in the pit of my stomach.

My eyes flutter shut sometimes during the movie. They blink open when I hear hushed voices, "Mom fell asleep," Connor says in a loud whisper. I immediately hear Carson, "Shh... don't wake her. She seemed tired." Then, "Okay," in another loud whisper from Connor.

My lips twitch, and then I slowly sit up, "I'm awake, guys."

Connor grins, "Mom, you fell asleep halfway through the movie."

I smile, "I guess I was more tired than I realized."

Carson frowns and gives me a look filled with concern. "You aren't coming down with something, are you?"

I automatically start to shake my head no and then hesitate. "You know, I had a headache earlier. That's probably why I've been feeling a little drained."

I see Carson's frown clear. He reaches down and pulls me up beside him.

"Why don't you go to bed early? Maybe that will help," the concern in his voice, doing a number on my already over-whelmed emotions.

I draw in a shaky breath. "Yeah, that's a good idea. I'm sure I'll feel better tomorrow." I inwardly wince at my words.

In the bedroom, I get ready for bed. The comfort of the thin cotton feels reassuring against my skin. I crawl between the cool sheets and fall asleep almost as soon as my head hits the pillow.

Twenty-Seven

Carson

It's the end of the week. I grimace as I glance at the clock. It's another late night at the office. I force my attention back to the handful of people sitting around the wide conference table. Its mahogany surface is polished to a high shine that gleams from the fluorescent lights above.

"Gentlemen, is there anything else we need to discuss, or can we conclude the meeting?"

I see nods of relief as briefcases are snapped open and chairs are scraped back. I give a cynical smile. They didn't get exactly what they wanted, but neither did I. I held firm in the face of their joint opposition. In the long run, I secured another two years with our biggest client.

Knight Security is massive. Even though we're headquartered in Jacksonville, we have clients all over the country; we take care of their every security need. We monitor and maintain their security cameras and any surveillance. Two years ago, we agreed to partner on some software with Val's family company, Carlucci Software, and that was a strategic move. It placed us in a superior position over the competition.

As the door shuts behind the last person, I stand up and stretch, the familiar ache in my lower back, a dull throb. This is the third time this week that I've been caught at the office for one reason or another.

A victory for Knight Security, but the satisfaction feels hollow. I shake my head at the irony. There was a time when I would rather be at work than at home.

Now, with Anna and Connor, I almost resent the time away from them. These late nights feel like stolen moments. Some CEO I am, I think with a laugh. But I know that the early years of ceaseless effort have put the company in an enviable position. Now, it practically runs itself. Well, almost, I admit, with a smirk.

I reach for the familiar, worn leather of my briefcase—home beacons, more alluring than the thrill of closing this deal.

The apartment's silence lets me know that everyone is already in bed. I softly walk through the dimly lit rooms and approach Connor's bed. I quietly open the door and look over at him. I was only going to check on him, but the quiet, rhythmic sound of his breathing lures me forward.

I walk into his room and then settle into the armchair. I lean my head wearily back against its plush back and close my eyes as I listen to the contented sound of my son's breathing.

My son. Even now, it brings a smile to my face. Living my life as a bachelor I had no idea of the joy and contentment that a child could bring. And Anna, even though I sit here, there's a part of me that won't be satisfied until I pull her warm body up against my chest. Only then do I fall into a deep sleep.

She warms my bed and my heart. I'm torn because I crave a deeper connection with her, but I shudder at the thought of marriage. But what future do we have together, if not marriage?

I guess we could keep the status quo, but... I shake my head. I want the vows. I want a woman, a wife that I can trust—someone who will stand beside me through thick and thin, rich or poor. I give a bitter, silent laugh as I recognize the familiar words. They're marriage vows. Sickness or in health. Dammit! They mean something. How could she just ignore them? Knowing they mean nothing to her cuts deep, like a sharp knife.

Can I offer her marriage feeling the way I do? I grimace. My feelings run deep. I hesitate to think about the word love... but I know what we have feels right. She's everything I ever wanted in a partner. The sex is phenomenal and off the charts. Hell, even the way she cooks and cares for me and Connor is more than I ever dreamed. She just plain cares.

I'm sure being married to such an older man wasn't easy. Her sexual appetites match mine. For now, we'll live together and raise our son. That will have to be enough; I can't offer her anything more. A heavy sigh escapes my lips. Decision made, I wearily stand and make my way into the master bedroom.

Anna lies curled on her side, her knees drawn up to her stomach. Her chestnut hair lies like a dark banner against the white sheets. Her dark lashes against her pale skin make her look young, like a child. My eyes travel over her body, visible beneath the thin white nightgown.

As I observe her lush form, I give a smug smile. Definitely not a child. No, a grown woman. My eyes trace the firm curve of her hip: her bronze thigh and shapely leg peek out from beneath the covers. My eyes travel back up to her breasts as they push against the top of her nightgown. I know the weight of them as they fill my hands.

I'm suddenly hard and aching. My cock throbs with need. I quietly undress and crawl naked between the sheets. I reach out and pull Anna back against my bare chest. I have a moment's hesitation as I think of the dark circles under her eyes, she's seemed so exhausted lately. Then she stirs restlessly in my arms, pushing her firm bottom against my stiff erection.

My hands reach around to her front as I grope her breasts through the thin nightgown. I feel them pebble at my touch. One minute, she's asleep; the next, she's giving a low moan as she pushes back against me. Her need matches my own. I grab the hem of her nightgown and pull it up around her waist, baring her smooth, firm ass.

Keeping her back to me, I lift her thigh and slide between her legs. My cock is eager to probe into her warm core. I hold back, reaching down to see if she's ready for me. I slowly push in a finger, knuckle deep. She squirms restlessly, and I feel her wetness.

I silently slip into her slick folds from behind, pulling her toward me until I'm in, to the hilt. I pause for a moment -

feeling like I've come home. I squeeze her breasts through the fabric as they fill my hands. Then they travel back to her hips as I anchor them and begin to slowly but steadily stroke into her.

I slowly increase the pace but maintain my steady strokes even as I grit my teeth to stay the course. I feel her flutter, the beginnings of a tremor, and then she unexpectedly shatters in my arms. I hold her until she's finished, and then it's my turn as I pump in and out a few more times, and just as unexpectedly, I climax, filling her.

I hold her as our breathing slows. I lean my head down and kiss the top of her head, her hair. This is probably the first time I've made love to her silently. Not a word was spoken. I can tell she's already fallen back to sleep. I stay connected to her while I hold her. I realize my word choice. Made love. Yes, this felt like more than just sex. It felt like making love... with Anna.

I fall asleep with my arms wrapped around her, holding her close against my heart.

It's morning when I open my eyes. My arms are empty, and I'm alone in the bed. I lay there for a moment or two listening. It takes a minute to realize it's the weekend. I don't need to jump up and get to the office. I grin and then stretch lazily. I hear the familiar theme song of the SpongeBob Square Pants and have to smile. There's a part of me that misses not being in the living room sharing this special moment with my son.

But there's another part of me that wants a long, hot shower. I hear the front door being opened and an exchange of voices. Then the door closes. I frown. I start to sit up when the bedroom door opens, and Anna walks in, a sly grin on her face. She's dressed in her nightgown from last night with a robe over it.

I lean back in the bed and prop my hands under my head. "Who was at the door?" My voice curious.

Anna gives me a slow, sexy smile. "Your mom. She picked up Connor to take him to the Museum of Science of History. She'll drop him off later this afternoon." She then takes off her robe and nightgown. My eyes admire her slender form and sweet curves.

My grin grows to mirror Anna's, "Later this afternoon?" She nods, "That's right."

I reach out and snag her hand, then I give a careful jerk, and she lands on my chest with a soft gasp. My arms instantly wrap around her, trapping her against my body. She doesn't try to escape. Instead, I feel her lips begin to trace my tribal tattoo softly.

"I was thinking we could take a long hot shower, but now, I'm thinking we can wait. Until after."

She looks up at me coyly, "After what?"

I roll until she's under me. Nudging her legs apart with my thigh, I settle in between them.

"This," I groan as I enter her in one powerful stroke.

Anna pours me another cup of coffee and she sips her morning tea. We've spent most of the morning in bed and in the large shower. Taking Anna when she's wet and soapy started the day off right. It's a routine I could get used to.

I rub my full stomach, "Breakfast was delicious. Thank you." She smiles at my sincere compliment. She always seems surprised when I thank her for cooking.

I lean back in my chair and say with a smirk, "Great food, great sex. A man could get used to waking up like this every day." I say it with a teasing smile, but I'm only half joking.

I see her smile falter, and I frown, "What's wrong, Anna?"

She turns toward me with a hesitant smile, "Carson. I wanted to talk to you about... our future."

Instantly, I feel my defenses rise, and my face hardens. I try to hide my knee-jerk reaction to her question as I feel her eyes study me. "Go on," I mutter softly, not knowing if I want to stop her or not.

She licks her lips and then says faintly, "I guess I wondered if you feel we have a future together. As a couple and as a family."

"We already are a family, Anna. Regardless of any label." I see a shadow cross her eyes, and it leaves me feeling on edge.

"So, um... our relationship. Do you want any more children?" She asks softly.

I suddenly sit up straight as my eyes narrow on her face. "Are you asking about marriage, Anna?"

"No, not really. I'm trying to find out how you feel about children and—"

"I don't," I say firmly. She gives a confused frown, "You don't... what? You wouldn't want another child."

I stand up and pace, "I don't want to get married. I don't want the institution of marriage. Not with you—" When she winces, I try to quantify it, "Anna, I just... I'm not ready to offer marriage yet. Not now... maybe not ever. I don't know. So, for now. No. I don't want to even think about having another child." Her eyes darken with emotion from the pain my words inflict.

Walking back to the table, I slide into my chair. "I'm sorry if that hurts you. I don't mean to—"

"No, I... I understand, Carson," she stammers, but I see the wounded deer look in her eyes.

I lean forward, "Anna. I have feelings for you. I just don't know about all the rest right now. Let's just enjoy what we have. Okay?"

She looks like I'm breaking her heart. Dammit, if I'm honest, that's how I feel right now, too, like someone is tearing my heart out by the roots. "Anna, I'm sorry. I'm just not ready..."

She nods, but I see the tears welling in her eyes, and then one spills over and runs down her cheek. I swear it feels like a red-hot poker to my chest. She jumps up and then runs out of the room.

I sit there feeling like a jerk, a fool. A lovesick fool. I pull away from the table and then drop my head in my hands. I love you, Anna. Why can't I forget the past and admit my feelings to her?

Why can't I tell her that I love her? Because then she'd want me to marry her... and I'm not ready for that yet.

What started as a wonderful day spent making love now feels torn apart by her anguish.

I turn to follow Anna, but my footsteps slow and then halt. I need to give her some space.

Turning, I grab up keys; then I stop again. I should at least leave her a note. I walk over to the counter and get the pad of paper and a pen. I write. 'Anna, I didn't mean to hurt you. I'm going out. I'll be back later.' I pause with the pen in my hand. I want to write Love, Carson. But I can't tell her like this. Instead, I sign it, 'Carson.'

Then, with a heavy heart, I walk out the door. It shuts with an ominous click behind me.

Twenty-Eight

Anna

A crushing weight settles in my chest, squeezing the air from my lungs. I feel like my heart is breaking. A sob escapes my lips. This can't be good for the baby.

With tears blurring my vision, I stumble into our bedroom and collapse on the bed. I curl into a fetal position. I pull my knees against my chest. My right hand instinctively lands on my abdomen, a silent connection with the tiny life growing inside me.

"It's okay, baby," I whisper, my voice thick with emotion, "I love you, and your Daddy will love you too. I know he will." A tear slides down my face, "He... he just can't quite forgive me yet. But little one, I know he'll love you. I know he will..."

I hug my knees tighter, and as I rock back and forth on the bed, the rhythmic motion is an attempt to soothe the emotions that course through me. Exhaustion eventually claims me. When I open my eyes, they feel gritty. I'm still curled up in the bed, the sheets in a tangle around me.

Pulling in a ragged breath, I sit up on the side of the bed. Then I wearily make my way into the bathroom and splash cold water on my face.

As I dry my face, I glance in the mirror. The reflection that stares back is a stranger, a woman consumed by worry. My tears have washed away any facade, leaving behind the raw vulnerability of my emotions.

I'm an ugly crier; my lids are swollen, and my cheeks are stained red from my hot tears. And I'm not done! I suddenly bring the towel up and drop my face into it. Fresh tears squeeze out of my eyes in a silent torrent. Really? I think cynically, haven't I shed enough tears already?

The phone rings, shattering the quiet of the room. I frown, completely forgetting where I left it. I rush to the kitchen, scooping it up, as the screen flashes my mother-in-law's name.

"Bonnie?" I manage, my voice shaky.

"Hi, Anna," she says cheerfully. "No worries, I just called to see if I could keep Connor overnight. Some friends of mine asked me over for dinner. Their grandson, who's the same age as Connor, is visiting. I thought it would be nice to bring Connor along. He could spend the night at my house."

Relief washes over me. "That's fine, Bonnie," I manage to get out.

"Great! Maybe you and Carson could come over for lunch tomorrow? Around one?"

"Um... yeah, that might work out," I hedge. "Carson's not here right now, but he can call you if that doesn't work."

"Alright, Anna. Oh, Connor wants to say hi." I hear a shuffling sound, and then Connor's excited voice fills my ear. "Hey, Mom. I'm spending the night with grandma. Can we go out on the boat tomorrow?"

"I'm not sure, honey," I say, "but if we can, I'll bring your swimsuit. Okay?"

"Cool. Thanks, Mom!" His voice fades as Bonnie takes the phone back.

The call ends, and I stand there staring down at the phone in my hand, a wave of exhaustion washing over me.

I sink onto the stool at the kitchen counter. Seeing Carson's note, I pull it toward me and read it. I sigh; the weight of my secret feels heavier than ever. I scold myself. I should have just told Carson about the baby. Instead, I wanted to test the waters first. A way to gauge his openness about having another child. Ridiculous. And it wasn't fair.

Haven't I learned that lesson? I should have just started with the truth, plain and simple: 'Carson, I'm pregnant. The baby is yours. I'm sorry, but we were careless, and the blame falls on both of us. And ... and... I love you.' No, I can't confess my feelings for him yet.

A surge of anger replaces my self-pity. Here I am, wallowing in my misery while the baby inside me needs me to be strong. This is not the end of the world. I still need to tell him, just... just not today. I think cowardly.

The sudden opening of the front door startles me. Carson stands in the doorway. He has Graham's bright yellow box in his hands. My stomach muscles tighten. My eyes widen with alarm.

He sets the box down on the dining room table. I stand up and slowly approach him; I'm practically holding my breath.

He simply looks at me. "Carson, I guess you know about..." I trail off as he approaches, a tender warmth in his eyes that stops me mid-sentence.

"Anna, I went to the storage room," he explains softly. "I wanted to get the fishing gear... I knocked over this box."

"It's Graham's," I reply softly. "He kept all his legal papers and journals in here."

Carson nods. "Yes. His journals. Have you ever read them?"

"Me? No, they were his." I look up at Carson with a frown. "I know you don't want me to talk about him—"

"No, Anna. It's okay. I know the truth now," he says gently.

"You do? Then you know that he only married me because the lawyer recommended it. Neal... Neal would have..."

Carson comes up and cradles me in his arms. "Neal could have contested the will and then gambled it all away," he murmurs. I lean against him, a wave of relief washing over me. Finally, we're discussing Graham and the past. Maybe we can then put it behind us.

"Anna, I'm a stubborn fool for not letting you explain," he admits. "But, did you know that Graham wanted me to read the journals? He left them for me."

I frown up at Carson, confused. "What, No. I... He never told me. He just asked me to keep them. I thought maybe he wanted Connor to read them, so I thought I'd give them to Connor when he was older."

"No, Anna. Graham wrote the journals for me. I'm the hot-headed guy who left you pregnant. I'm sure he meant them for me."

"What do they say?" I ask him, curiosity in my gaze.

"Well, the main thing they told me is that you refused to exchange wedding vows," he replies. "He wrote that they were too important to you. You didn't feel right saying vows, or wearing white, or even a wedding dress. You refused his ring. You also didn't want to be married in a church."

Carson gives a rueful laugh. "He really admired you for your beliefs." He pulls me away from his chest and stares down into my eyes. "And so do I, Anna."

In a low voice, he explains, "The fact that you wouldn't make any vows says a lot about your character." He continues, "I feel the same way. Wedding vows... they're sacred. Something that should only be shared between two people who are in love with each other. Graham quoted your words, Anna. For me. He wanted me to know."

I look up at Carson, yearning for more. "What else did he say?"

Carson sighs. "Anna, I've been sitting down in the storage room since I left the apartment. When the box toppled over, I didn't even want to touch it. Connor said the yellow box was Graham's." He shakes his head as he admits, "I'm so glad I did. One of the journals fell open. It's almost like Graham was in the room with me, forcing me to read them."

"The first journal talked about how he felt about you as a child," he begins. "How your parents and he and his wife, Martha, were so close. He talked about Neal and how they hoped he could fight his gambling addiction and then their disappointment when he couldn't. Graham went on to describe himself as your doting uncle."

I smile. "Yes. Oh my God, Carson. He always told me I was family. Did he say anything about his condition?"

"Oh yes, I think that was journal four, but Anna, the journals were more about you," he clarifies. "How you nursed him through it all. How badly he felt about taking your youth." Then Carson laughs. "How, if he had felt better, he'd have hunted me down and demanded I listen to reason and marry you."

He squeezes me tight, and my tears again start to flow. I look up at Carson. "I loved him like an uncle, Carson. There was never anything more," I finish, my voice trembling slightly.

Carson nods, his gaze searching mine. "I know, Anna. He told me. He loved his late wife, and they both thought of you as their own." He reaches into his pocket and pulls out a worn photograph; the edges softened with time. "He had this picture pressed in between the pages. It's you as a child, with him and his wife. He has his arm around you, and you're nestled in his arms. I swear I can see the love in your eyes, and he wrote that they were always so proud of you."

A bittersweet smile graces my lips. "Yes, I had won a Spelling Bee that day. I remember wearing that red sweater."

"Yeah," Carson continues, his voice filled with newfound warmth. "He also talked about how your father made some bad financial decisions, and he was just getting on his feet when they died. He talked about how he was helping you find a place to live, but you insisted on taking care of him. He felt terrible about you having to spend your days taking care of a..." he hesitates, searching for the right word.

"A crotchety old man," I reply with a soft laugh, wiping away a stray tear. "That's what he called himself. Oh, Carson, he was so kind to me. You, you would have liked him."

"I do like him, Anna," Carson replies, his eyes filled with sincerity. "There's so much more, but that's the highlight. Some of the journals were about Connor and how he felt selfish because he had the joy of seeing Connor grow. You gave him something to live for."

Carson takes my face in his hands, turning it so our eyes meet. "Anna, I love you. I'm in love with you. I started falling for you eleven years ago, and I haven't stopped."

His words hang in the air, heavy with emotion. My heart thrums in my chest; it's deafening to hear the silence that has settled around us.

"Carson," I whisper, my voice thick with emotion, "I love you too."

Carson grins at me, "Graham said you did. He said I was a damn fool for not seeing that for myself."

He leans down, his lips brushing softly against mine. The kiss is gentle, filled with a lifetime of unspoken words and desires. It feels like a promise, a new beginning for us both.

He pulls back slightly, his forehead resting against mine. "There's something else," he murmurs, his voice husky.

"What is it?" I ask, my breath catching in my throat.

He reaches into his pocket again, this time pulling out an old velvet box. My breath catches in my throat as I recognize it. Graham had bought me a ring, which I refused.

Carson opens the box, revealing a delicate platinum ring adorned with a single sparkling diamond. "Anna," he begins, his voice trembling slightly, "these were Graham's instructions. He left this ring for when I proposed. He wanted you to have it. He wrote that I was a fool and should have married you a long time ago."

Tears well up in my eyes again. "Oh, Carson," I whisper, overwhelmed with emotion.

"Anna," he continues, "the journals... they opened my eyes. They showed me the man I could have been, the man you deserved. I may not be perfect, but I want to be that man for you."

Carson kneels on one knee, "Will you marry me, Anna? Because you love me, and I love you?"

I stare at the ring, the diamond twinkling as it catches the light, reflecting my emotions back at me. This feels so right, so real, a dream come true.

A slow smile spreads across my face. "Yes, Carson," I say, my voice thick with emotion. "Yes, I'll marry you."

He stands, letting out a deep sigh, a mixture of joy and disbelief washing over his face. He slips the ring onto my finger, and it fits perfectly.

I pull his head down toward mine and kiss him. When he raises his head, tears are still shimmering in my eyes. I wipe them away with the back of my hand, and his thumbs gently follow suit, brushing away the last traces. He leans down, placing soft kisses on my cheeks, erasing the salty tracks with his lips. My heart feels like it's overflowing with love.

When he finally steps back and grins down at me, I search his face, a mix of emotions swirling within me. My gaze flickers to the yellow box on the table. "Carson, is that all you found in there?" I want no secrets between us.

His smile falters slightly. "Why, was there something else?"

I meet his gaze, a hesitant smile playing on my lips. "You didn't find a bag filled with pamphlets?"

He furrows his brow. "Pamphlets?" A flicker of realization dawns on him. "Oh, yeah. When I finished the last journal, there was a bag filled with a bunch of old pregnancy pamphlets. I don't know why Graham held on to those."

I bite my lip, forcing down a nervous flutter in my stomach. "Carson, those aren't old. I put them in there yesterday."

His frown deepens momentarily before slowly starting to curve up. "Yesterday?" He takes a step closer, connecting the dots quickly.

I nod, unable to hold back a tear that rolls down my cheek. "Yes. I went to see the doctor, and he confirmed... I'm pregnant."

The realization hits him like a wave. Joy floods his face, erasing any trace of confusion. He pulls me into a tight embrace, his arms wrapping protectively around me. Then, he pulls back, letting out a laugh.

"Cream cheese! I should have figured it out," he exclaims. "Graham mentioned you were craving cream cheese and... crying a lot."

A blush creeps up my neck. "Well, some things never change, I guess."

His hand comes out, and he places it gently over my abdomen, a tender smile on his face.

"Carson, you look happy about it. You are happy, right?" I need to hear the words.

His smile grows, his eyes shining with a mix of excitement and love. "Can't you tell? I'm ecstatic! This time, I won't miss a moment. I'll be there for you every step of the way. I'll get to see you swollen with our child." He lands a kiss on my eyes, my nose, and my cheeks before he continues, "I'll be with you for the doctor's appointments."

His voice continues to warm, "We'll set up the nursery together, and I'll be here to massage your swollen feet and wipe away every tear... happy or not." The tender words - a promise.

His arms tighten around me as he tilts my face upward, my lips to his. I'm breathless when he finally raises his head. I see the familiar flicker of desire in his gaze, but this time, it's laced with a tenderness that sends shivers down my spine. His kisses turn passionate. The hunger is undeniable, but there's a sweetness to it now, a promise of a future built on love and shared dreams.

He pulls away reluctantly, a glance at the clock reminding him of the time. "So, when's Mom supposed to drop off Connor?"

I raise an eyebrow, a knowing smile gracing my lips. "Bonnie called. She's keeping Connor overnight. We're invited for lunch tomorrow."

"Overnight, huh?" he muses, a husky quality creeping into his voice.

I can't help but laugh at his sudden shift in focus. Before I have a chance to catch my breath, I feel myself being swept off my feet. He carries me towards our bedroom.

The promise of a passionate evening hangs heavy in the air. This time, however, it's filled with a new layer of anticipation, the excitement of starting our new family together.

Carson enters the bedroom, heat smoldering in his eyes as he looks down at me, cradled in his strong arms. He gives me a wicked, sexy grin, then turns and kicks the door shut.

Epilogue

Anna

Carson unlocks the door, and I enter our new home. We moved in four months ago, wanting to be settled before the baby arrived. So far, we're loving the additional space, and Connor loves having a backyard. Carson set up a basketball hoop, and he's been helping Connor with his free-throw shot.

As we step into the foyer, my appreciative gaze takes in the spacious open living space. It feels perfect for our growing family.

Bonnie stands on the upstairs landing, greeting us. "Welcome home." She explains, "The children are fine. Connor is watching over Gracie in her crib."

Carson and I both walk to the stairs and make our way to the nursery.

Bonnie asks, "You're home early. How was date night?" with a twinkle in her eye.

As a smile blooms over my face. "It was wonderful," I admit with a glance toward Carson.

"Yes, it was. Thanks, Mom." Then, with a rueful shake of his head, he says, "We only texted you twice to check in on the baby."

Entering the room, Bonnie proudly states, "Connor has been watching over her since you left. He's quite the protective big brother."

The nursery has pale pink walls and is decorated with prints of fluffy lambs and bunnies on the walls. It's filled with dark wood furniture. In the corner stands the crib. I spot Connor hovering over our baby girl. Our voices must have woken her because her eyes flutter open.

Carson reaches down and gently picks her up. "Hey, Princess. Did you miss us?" She gives him a toothless grin. Connor asks with an eager look in his eyes, "Dad, can I hold her?" Carson answers, "Sure, Son. See if you can rock her back to sleep." Connor goes to the rocking chair, and Carson places the baby in his arms.

Bonnie and I stand watching. I feel her arm go around me. I get a lump in my throat as I watch Carson place Gracie Rose into Connor's eager arms. After Connor carefully supports her head, Carson steps back.

Gracie's eyes blink open wide, and her chubby little arms wave with delight when Connor whispers, "Gracie, it's me. Your big brother." He cradles her safely in his arms.

As I observe the love and devotion that shines out of Connor's eyes, I have to blink the moisture from mine. Gracie, with her dark fuzz hair and cloudy blue eyes, is enthralled with Connor, and he's fascinated with her.

When Bonnie approaches the rocking chair, Carson turns and walks toward me. He wraps his arm around my waist and pulls me against his side as we watch Connor, who continues to coo at Gracie. She loves the attention and gives a big smile, a dimple showing in her cheek.

"Look, she has dimples!" Connor says, excitement and awe in his voice. Carson gives me a squeeze, and I turn my eyes to his. "Anna, I can't imagine my life without you and our children." He turns me toward him and gives me a loving kiss.

We hear Connor say, "She's already going back to sleep." Bonnie smiles as she takes the baby out of Connor's arms and places her back in the crib.

We all quietly walk out of the nursery and down the stairs. Connor disappears into the kitchen while Carson walks his mother to the door. "Mom, thanks for watching the kids tonight."

Our wedding picture catches my eye. It is a snapshot of pure happiness: me, glowing in my gown, and Carson, his gaze radiating love and pride. One arm embraces me close, and his other hand rests protectively on Connor's shoulder, standing proudly by his father's side.

I smile as I remember that day... Connor walked me down the aisle, looking like a miniature of his father in a matching tuxedo, his hair slicked back. The wedding march music filled the air.

That's when I looked up and saw Carson standing tall at the altar. His gaze locked onto mine, and for a moment, it was just us two. The rest of the world melted away.

His intense blue eyes shimmered with a love so profound it took my breath away.

Finally, I reached him, and he took my hand in his. The warmth of his touch sent a shiver through me. In that moment, I saw not just the handsome man I fell in love with years ago but the man he'd become—a man tempered by time, his eyes now filled with trust and devotion.

We repeated the wedding vows softly but with a purpose. Each word a sacred pledge. The raw emotion in Carson's eyes spoke volumes. Those vows were more than words; they were a testament to the journey we'd shared. Our love had endured and flourished even in the harshest of conditions...

"Anna, Honey, you okay?" Carson's voice brings me back to the present. To the now.

I nod, glancing again at the photo. "Carson, that moment in the church was so perfect. My happily ever after come true."

I feel cherished as he wraps me in his arms, laughs, and dips me back to kiss me like he did during our wedding.

He promises, "Anna, every moment we spend together is our happily ever after."

The End.

Did you like this Book?

Then you'll love: Fake Marriage to the Billionaire

A fake marriage with the billionaire next door seems simple. What's complicated is finding out I'm having his baby.

My inheritance comes with a cruel ultimatum - get a husband by my 25th birthday or lose everything.

Enter my billionaire next-door neighbor and (until now) strictly platonic best friend.

His solution: a temporary fake marriage.

I get my inheritance and he gets to feel like a hero. Perfect.

Except living under the same roof with those steely blue eyes and chiseled abs that melt panties is doing a number on our "just friends" policy.

Fake kisses feel real, and late-night talks turn into stolen moments that leave me breathless.

The lines blur, friendship morphing into something hotter, and definitely forbidden.

He's soon warming my heart and my bed.

It's a delicious danger, a fast burn that threatens to consume everything.

But our deal has an expiration date. One year and our fake marriage is supposed to end.

Now, two pink lines might change everything.

Start reading Fake Marriage to the Billionaire NOW!

Sneak Peek - Chapter One

Chase

I rumble up to the curb on my Harley, the address Val gave me burning a hole in my pocket. Urgent, she said. Emergency, she insisted. And now, here I am, scanning the street, but she's nowhere in sight. A church looms on the corner, its solemn presence mocking my confusion. She said to meet her at the corner of Hendricks and—

Damn! Now I see her, she's rushing toward me in a... wedding dress? It's white and has miles of ruffles. It sure looks like a wedding dress, it screams 'bride'.

Val has ample curves and wild, curly black hair. She has big, soulful, dark eyes and usually a wide, friendly smile.

I consider her my closest friend, thus off-limits. Val has a heart of gold. Which is why, right now, I'm reeling. Why is she wearing a wedding dress and running away from a church? Unless she is getting married... or was.

For a second, I'm frozen, my mind racing with a thousand questions.

I knew she was dating some guy, but she never talked about him much. I didn't think the relationship was serious. The one time I met him, he seemed like a condescending prick, and I didn't like how he treated Val. I remember telling her she needed to ditch him. I've only been gone for three months. My heart hammers against my ribs as I wonder what the hell is going on here.

She's close enough now that I can see the desperation etched on her face, an apologetic smile flickering across her lips as she leaps onto the bike. "Go, Chase! Go!" she pleads, and I don't need telling twice.

We tear down the street, the roar of my engine drowning out the shouts of the couple emerging from the church, their arms flailing in the air as they watch us drive away.

A few blocks later, Val's body presses against mine, her breath hot on my leather jacket. "Thank you, Chase. I think we've lost them," she whispers, and the weight of her forehead against my back is heavier than any words.

As I drive us down the road, we get mixed reactions from everyone we pass. Some people walking on the sidewalk shout congratulations. Meanwhile, others in their cars honk their horns. I'm wearing my black Harley biker leathers, and Val is wearing a white ruffled wedding dress on the back of my Harley. It's not a sight you see every day.

I think about the girl on the back of my bike; my friend is a computer programmer. She never fusses with her hair, as her unruly dark curls wouldn't behave anyway. She rarely wears makeup but doesn't need to, as she has a natural beauty. She's typically dressed in cut-off jeans and baggy shirts, but they can't hide her lush curves.

I'm unsure where Val wants me to take her, so I drive us home.

Val and I live in a large, older duplex. She lives on the left, and I live in a matching apartment on the right. I've known Val for almost two years now. She's a great neighbor because she never complains and a close friend.

The duplex is brick, like many of the homes in this area. It has moss growing up the side of the exterior. There are flower beds in the front of the duplex because Val planted them about a year ago. The flowers currently have bright red and yellow blooms. She told me the names of the plants, but I forget what they are, especially now when all I can picture is Val in that damn wedding dress.

I stop the bike on my side of the driveway. I keep it upright while Val climbs off the back.

She's standing there looking like someone just kicked her puppy. I take off my helmet.

"Val, is that a wedding dress?"

"Yes, I was supposed to get married today," there's a hitch to her voice.

"What? To that guy you were dating when I left? That prick? What did he do?"

"His name is Tony... and... I walked in on him and my bridesmaid, my cousin Cristina... having sex in his dressing room. An hour before the ceremony."

"Damn! That's brutal," I shake my head in disgust.

"Yeah."

"Are you okay?"

Val sniffles a couple of times. I hope she isn't going to cry.

"He probably just wanted my inheritance," she sighs, "I knew Tony wasn't really in love with me, but I thought... oh well, it doesn't matter."

"What do you mean?"

"I guess he planned on having an open marriage." She grimaces. "Listen, I don't want to stand out here where everyone can see me in this monstrosity of a dress."

"So, I take it you didn't pick the dress? It's hideous, by the way."

She ruefully looks down at the miles of ruffles, "No, my aunt and cousin planned the wedding. They picked out the church, my dress, the shoes, and, I think, maybe my groom."

"Come on. We'll go to my place. First, I want to pull my bike around back so no one can see it."

I get back on my bike and drive it around to the backyard. Our duplex is in the San Marco area of Jacksonville, Florida. We share the front and backyard. While the flower beds are all Val, I put in a fire pit and places to sit in our backyard. We have a place to entertain, and I purchased a huge grill and smoker.

I pull my bike into the backyard behind the house, near the grill.

I check to make sure the motorcycle is completely hidden from view from anyone who might drive by.

When I walk into my apartment, I see Val standing near my table, still in dress, and I hate that she still has that same sad look in her eyes.

"Why don't you sit down and tell me all about it?"

She looks at me with her big puppy dog brown eyes, "Okay."

322   DAMAGED GRUMPY BILLIONAIRE DADDY

She sits at the table while I walk to the kitchen, "I figure we need something to drink while we talk. I'll get you a diet coke, and I'll be right back."

I wanted to demand she tell me what the hell is going on, but one look at her face, and here I am, getting her a drink and being patient.

She gives a ghost of a smile as I pour her favorite drink over ice and hand it to her; then, I sit down with my drink.

"Okay, now tell me why your groom was banging your bridesmaid and why the hell you were getting married in the first place. Especially without telling me."

Do you like FREEBIE Romance books?

Want to know who started the Too Series?

Sign up for my newsletter and get IN TOO DEEP for FREE!

(Haley and Jake's Story)

H.O.T. Playboy Billionaire Needs Fake Fiancée!

She's off-limits, but I'm about to make her mine.

What could possibly go wrong?

The Company Board of Directors makes it clear: Clean up my act!

So, when I'm caught in a compromising position, I do the only thing I can think of, I lie and tell the world we're engaged.

But here's the kicker.

Haley isn't just any woman. She's my best friend's younger sister and completely off-limits.

Now, we're playing house, pretending to be madly in love.

Yet, the more I try to keep my distance, the more I find myself drawn to her infectious laughter and fiery spirit.

And the biggest problem?

I might just be falling for her, and if my lies unravel, I could lose everything, including the only woman who's ever made me want to be more than just a playboy.

Sign Up Now! for my Free Book and Newsletter or Scan the QR Code Below:

Free Book
& Newsletter Sign Up

Want to see the rest of my books? Click HERE! for my All Books Page or Scan the QR Code Below:

*All Books by
author Kelly
Thomas*

Sign up for my Newsletter to be notified when my next book in this series goes live: Sign Up NOW!or Scan the QR Code Below:

*Newsletter
Sign Up*

59037186R00186